Greta Garbo

The Woman I loved the Most

Armando G. Muñoz

Copyright © 2023

All Rights Reserved

Dedication

To,

Esther and Jesus,

Two of the people who put their trust in me,

and gave me all their support.

About the Author

Armando G. Muñoz is a Cuban writer, who was born in Havana, Cuba, on November 17, 1957. Graduated from the Marianao Institute of Economics. He worked in multiple state institutions, always dedicated to economic activity.

While he lived on the island, he never wrote a complete work, for fear of losing the opportunity to escape from his homeland, he destroyed notes and annotations, which he had no one to leave with.

It was in the cold winter nights of New Jersey, when he wrote his first work, "Absolve me, it doesn't matter, history will condemn me", continued by the novels "Gilda", "Greta Garbo, the Woman I Loved the most", the short stories "Morbid Words", "Memories and Retellings", the collections of poems "You, my utopia", "The yellow rose", among other works.

At the moment he has finished the novels; "When memories bleed", "For Love, from Mario to Maria", the collections of poems "In the Wind of New York" and "Awakening your skin", a collection of stories titled "The Contract".

All these works are written in Spanish..

Preface

In the annals of history, there exist names that refuse to fade into obscurity. One such luminous figure is Greta Garbo. She graced the silver screen with unparalleled brilliance during Hollywood's silent film era, forever enshrouded in an aura of mystique. Despite retiring at the tender age of 35 after a remarkable career spanning 28 films, her memory endures and is cherished by cinephiles worldwide.

In the pages of this compelling novel, guided by the poignant monologues of Mercedes Acosta, a poet and actress who shared an ardent, clandestine friendship and love affair with Greta Garbo for three decades, Armando G. Muñoz unveils a lesser-known facet of the iconic actress.

It is imperative to recollect the societal norms of the 1930s and 1940s, when any form of female erotic attraction, particularly lesbianism, was relentlessly condemned and relegated to the shadows. These women had no recourse but to conceal even the most subtle hints of their affections.

Born in 1893 to a Cuban father and a Spanish mother, Mercedes Acosta, over the course of her life, donned the roles of actress, poet, and novelist, albeit with limited success in the latter pursuit. Nevertheless, she remains indelibly etched in history due to her passionate liaisons with luminaries of Hollywood and Broadway, including the iconic actress Marlene Dietrich and the renowned dancer Isadora Duncan. Mercedes is perhaps best remembered for her declaration, *"There are no impossible women, only difficult women."*

Yet, it is Mercedes' tempestuous and tumultuous relationship with Greta Garbo that looms largest in the archives of her life. Their fateful encounter in 1921 quickly spiraled into a passionate love affair that would endure for years.

As Mercedes neared the end of her life in 1960, she penned her memoirs in a poignant volume titled "Here Lies the Heart." However, at the time of its release, her revelations of intimate relationships, especially her liaisons with Acosta, challenged the societal norms of the era, leading many prominent figures to vehemently deny their veracity.

In "Greta Garbo: The Woman I Loved the Most," Armando Muñoz masterfully delves into the intricacies of Mercedes de Acosta's enigmatic persona and her profound obsessions, chief among them being Greta. Through impeccable prose and meticulous attention to detail, Muñoz offers a vivid and revealing narrative, elevating this book beyond the cacophony of modern literature. In an age inundated with countless volumes, this one stands as a compelling testament to a remarkable story that deserves your attention.

Ismael Lorenzo

"Life would be so wonderful,

if we only knew

what to do with it."

–Greta Garbo

For Greta,

For all the love you made me feel,

You belong to me.

Some things belong to others,

for there is no other way.

Why not let us then say,

for example,

salt to the sea,

a bird to the sky,

and you to me,

–Mercedes De Acosta

(New York, 1944)

*S*ame to Jesus, she rose on the third day, like a sort of messianic vision. Similar to a slug leaving its shell, she emerged from her lethargic state.

Without saying a word, she dressed herself in clothes that had been ironed and washed with infinite tenderness. I waited for the moment in which she would rid me of mine, my clothes that had dressed her in these past unforgettable days.

I watched with great devotion each of her steps as she put on sunglasses that hid her, which on this particular day seemed rather mournful—and her ample hat that hid most of her face, though she often used to say that *"Custom made Italian hats were not designed to hide oneself,"* or maybe she was being honest when she said she *"could not stand the sun."*

Either way, one could not deny that she had developed a lifelong habit of living like a shadow. Always aiming to go unnoticed by the surrounding world.

She lit up her cigarette, accompanied by fear—her lifelong mate—she walked to the door, leaving me no choice but to follow her and her silence close behind.

Before leaving, she turned to me and grazed her long and cold fingers over my face in what she meant as a loving gesture. Coldheartedly, she muttered three words that would become our epitaph, three words that created a schism between us and separated us worlds apart.

I couldn't imagine this would be the last time I'd see her. It didn't seem possible for me to even think, *"I wouldn't speak to her again."*

"I'll call you," She said in a whisper as she turned, almost disappearing at the elevator door.

Mom always spoke in a nostalgic manner about her own mother's recollections, those memories that went all the way back to the Spanish Court, to royal families during the Spanish Monarchy at the beginning of the nineteenth century. Her closest relative used to always say, *"Our*

Grandmother was a close cousin to María del Pilar Teresa Cayetano de Silva and Álvarez Toledo, the thirteenth Duchess of Alba."

Yes, the notorious and world-renowned Duchess of Alba, better known for inspiring *"La Maja Desnuda"* and *"La Maja Vestida"* by Francisco de Goya. Our aunt had gained her fame due to multiple romantic affairs during the reign of the strict and catholic Spanish Monarchy.

Inquisition mentality was still going strong, and you could be burnt at the stake with the mere accusation of practicing witchcraft or being a witch. This distant and unknown great-aunt died at 40 years old without leaving behind any descendants. She did, however, leave a good portion of her dowry to the son of the painter, who immortalized her through his paintings.

Our great–aunt did not include my grandmother in her will. Nonetheless, she did inherit us a great part of her folly and recklessness. She was capable of devising and carrying out the most outlandish adventures, from affairs with then–famous bullfighters to a particular air with a painter who would immortalize her in his portraits.

Manuel Godoy, one of the most affluent politicians of his time, became one of her better-known lovers. Desperately, he sought after the nude portrait of the Duchess, only to buy and keep it hidden behind a curtain. It was meant to only be enjoyed by him.

After dark, she would get dressed up as a common town girl and go out around town freely, enjoying an ordinary social life, a social life that would otherwise be out of reach for the noble duchess.

The Duchess of Alba made stops at the most popular pubs and would mingle with people she'd find there. People who, just like her, would go out in search of fun, drinks, and an overall good time. She lived inciting palatial gossip among everyone, envy among women, and desire among men.

Not least notorious was her rivalry with the Queen of Spain. Both prominent figures would compete to wear the most fashionable garments and accessories custom-made and ordered from Paris. The Duchess of Alba would ignite the fuel of their rivalry by dressing up her servants with the same garments the queen would use, just to laugh and mock her Highness.

This was the legacy left to our family.

The lack of evidence makes it easy to question whether we were indeed related. Nonetheless, and to dissipate any doubts, we still keep definite and conclusive proof of our birth and baptismal certificates. The facts speak for themselves.

Aida, Joaquín, Enrique, Ricardo, Angela, Maria, Rita, and myself, Mercedes de Acosta, are true descendants of the marriage between Ricardo de Acosta and Micaela Hernández de Alba and de Alba.

Our parents met when they had recently arrived in New York, both from very different walks of life. My father was a rich Cuban merchant who was stopped at Santiago for his participation and collaboration in the armed conflict between Creoles and the Spanish, who wished to keep Cuba as one of their many colonies.

With the help of friends and mates of the Libertarian Cause, my father managed to escape prison in Cuba. Once out of prison, he paid a hefty sum to a merchant boat captain to take him to Jamaica. Once having arrived in Kingston, he headed to New York, and the magical city enamored him. Soon after, he made the decision to make it his temporary home while still participating in activities held by fellow exiled Cubans who supported the revolutionary cause.

On the other hand, my mother was brought to New York for entirely different reasons. The once beautiful young Spanish girl came to the Big City looking for her scheming uncle, who, after stealing her fortune, fled to New York. After a long trial, she won the lawsuit against her devious uncle and luckily gained her fortune back.

Perhaps it was the will of God or destiny that allowed these two to meet and cross paths in the fast-moving city of New York. They both met at a friend's house during a casual party. Soon after being introduced, he asked her out to dance, and they danced the night away.

My parents were smitten with each other. They dated for a while and then quickly married. My parents agreed it was best for them to make New York their permanent home, where they had access to the best education and environment for their future family. Going back to Cuba was impossible for my father, and my mother was enamored with the city that was light years away from the archaic and dreary Madrid.

My siblings and I were born here and were raised as Catholics while we studied in American schools; we developed our character and decided who we would become in the future. We were all very different from one another. The man in my family lived a somber life, while the woman in my family—perhaps due to our great aunt's genes—made the Big City our royal court. We were a product of volatile love affairs and unstable homes shaken by unpredictable periods in life.

They bought an enormous house on Forty-Seventh St. between Fifth and Sixth Ave, just next door to the British Ambassador and very close to prominent figures, such as ex-president Teddy Roosevelt and William Vanderbilt.

My parents enjoyed being involved in the social engagements of the truly elite neighborhood. We were lucky enough to grow up surrounded by literature in a wealthy aristocratic environment, raised by educated Spanish aristocrats, rich Cuban landowners stricken by war, troubled uncles burdened by depression, and suicidal tendencies.

Our home was a constant in and out of relatives and friends. They arrived for the day and left after many years had gone by; many just walked out after having stayed for long periods with us, and others, well, unfortunately, others were carried out of our home in caskets.

Suicides were very common in our family. My father, *"the soldier"* as I used to call him, succumbed to his suicidal tendencies in 1907, during a period when he was affected by a severe depression.

A loud shot that resonated in each corner of our house shocked everyone and rushed us to our family library, the place where the sound came from.

There, sitting on his chair behind an enormous oak desk, with his chin placed on his chest while a bloodstream soaked his suit and destroyed his face.

When we found him, his hand was still on the smoldering hot revolver. This event left profound scars on the lives of my siblings and me. From the day of my birth, my world was shaken. I lived enclosed in my family's quirkiness. I was a child with no personality and no established gender.

Destiny and life had me be born as a girl, despite the desire of my father for a boy. Challenging the conventional social norm of the time, they dressed me as a boy and would call me Raphael at home.

And that's how my life started, regarding myself as a boy.

One unfortunate day, with the characteristically cruel innocence of kids, a boy told me, *"You're a young lady."*

I couldn't grasp the notion of being regarded as a woman. I dressed, acted, and thought like a boy. But, that day after he said that, it dawned on me that I couldn't change the fact that I was a woman, though it was a very difficult concept to assimilate. I still consider it the hardest and most painful revelation of my entire existence. It traumatized me. It didn't take long after for my mother to start dressing me as a girl and to call me by my name, *Mercedes*.

And like that, in just one day, I went from being a boy to a girl.

However, the damage was done. I was accustomed to regard myself as a boy.

Later, I became the subject of idle gossip among women in society. Had dressing me up as a boy turned me into a lesbian, or was I born a lesbian?

I don't know.

I have asked myself the same questions.

What if that bizarre period in my early childhood had influenced my sexual preferences, but then again, perhaps not?

Maybe I was born this way. It may be possible I loved women even while still in the womb.

Perhaps my father and mother had wished so intensely for a boy, and that's exactly what they got: a man trapped in a woman's body.

Undoubtedly, mothers have a sixth sense when it comes to their children's quirkiness. Early on, she noticed strange behaviors on my part. However, in order to avoid becoming the subject of harsh criticism among New York's elite, she decided to send me away to a French convent.

Fatal mistake, to say the least. Being amongst frustrated and repressed women, many in the same situation as me, just gave me the perfect platform to corroborate my sexual inclination as a lesbian.

Enveloped in the solitude of the cloister, away from indiscreet glares and my mother's overprotectiveness, I found myself in the perfect place for my development as an individual.

Among the novices, the nuns had their own private garden, the perfect hunting ground for young and inexpert ladies; there was plenty of time to choose the perfect virginal flower.

It was in this convent that I truly became myself.

It was where I broke the ties that bound me. It made me release my sails to the wind, and I wandered off to the appealing horizon. No one was there to stop it, not my mother, not my sibling, not even society.

I became addicted to the pleasures of the feminine body by touching them and enjoying them since the first time I became acquainted with them. My first encounter was with Cosette, a beautiful French girl from the cloister.

Like me, she had been sent away due *to "incorrigible deviations."* The moment we laid eyes on each other, we felt connected. There was no doubt she was wittier and more experienced than me, but just exchanging looks, we knew we were the same.

It all started as a game of becoming acquainted with one another. The first time we ran into each other in the bathrooms, before washing ourselves, we had to take off our habit. We weren't allowed to completely undress ourselves. We had to cover our bodies with our undergarments at all times.

While she slowly undressed before me, heightening my lust for her, I couldn't take my eyes off of her; it produced in me a strange but intriguing sensation. When she finally undressed, she went into the shower, leaving the door ajar.

A small gap allowed me to watch her completely naked. I admired her figure, her pale skin, her sinuous curves, and her luminous, perfect breasts with rose-colored aureoles. She looked at me and smiled. She knew what I felt in that moment. She knew the effect her naked body had on me.

There I was, sitting on the bench, half-dressed and desperately clenching part of my habit with my hands. I became paralyzed, completely hypnotized by the vision of the naked girl that stood before me. She placed herself in front of me, naked and unashamed, while she slid down her fingers on the surface of her moist skin until she started touching herself. Her tongue savored her lips, and her provocative green eyes were locked on me and enticed me to sin.

Sitting there, even without touching myself, I realized I couldn't resist the sexual desires within me. I felt drained, with barely any strength to move, much less to stand up. I watched how she continued to rub herself with her fingers and how her body quivered with the intense pleasure that overtook her. She finished bathing and continued to dress herself.

She came towards me, grabbed my face with her right hand, and whispered in my ear…

"I'll wait for you tomorrow; the best is yet to come…"

I do not know how long I sat there petrified when I finally woke from my lethargic state. I fail to remember if, indeed, I continued my bath. What I do know is that I couldn't take my eyes off the vision of Cosette naked while she touched herself before me. From that moment on, I was totally seduced.

In the solitude of my cell, I woke at night squirming like overtaken by a possessed person on my cot. My body suffered from fever. The sweat made my humid nightgown fool my sphincters into emptying my bladder. I slid my fingers on my inner thighs until I touched myself, until the humidity that wet my fingers was no longer urine, and the aroma that filled the room was that of green grapes.

Instinctively, I took my fingers to my mouth and savored them. They tasted like sour grapes drained with red wine.

I continued touching myself just like Cosette touched herself earlier that day.

It was a new discovery that I had made; the humidity and the desire intensified under the cast of my inexpert fingers.

I explored myself until encountering a small protuberance at the start of my vagina, a small button that, when touched by my fingers, would double its size sending electrifying sensations across my body. My hot outer lip swelled up due to the blood rushing in. Moments after touching myself, I relived the strange and pleasant sensation that lived in the bathroom while I looked at the girl.

We had more encounters after that, in the complicity of the bathrooms and the cloister, the garden, the rooms, and in each place within the convent where we ran into each other. Away from the stares of the nun, we exchanged kisses, sighs, and promises. I became addicted to her presence.

Had I found love with her?

Maybe I fell in love. Maybe it was just dependence. Cosette left the most wonderful mark in my memories. With her, I discovered my passion for sex. She was my teacher and my mentor. Clearly, she was well-studied in a subject I just began to discover.

Past the initial euphoria, the absurd and monotonous life in the convent continued to drag on. Sister Blanca, one of the nuns, took me under her spiritual guidance with the intention of turning me into her pupil. She took me along with her daily chores; we studied the scriptures together for hours. Nevertheless, something made me doubt her intentions; she was too loving, beyond what you would expect. Sister Blanca would look at me in a way that would make me blush.

Often, while I read, she listened. That is where I discovered her gaze upon me. I could feel her unnatural lust for me. When she felt my stare back, she felt exposed and would instantly start praying the rosary until her hands would give away her anxiety, she would smile, and her eyes would gleam with satisfaction.

One morning, when the bell rang announcing our morning prayer time, I faked a headache. I didn't want to come out of my cell. By dawn, I woke up aroused from a dream I had with Sister Blanca. I woke up in the middle of the night, prey to an incontrollable excitement, and I let loose my fingers and began to touch myself, playing in silence, biting my lips, muffling any moans. I had discovered in myself games, places where my sensations heightened by touch.

When my body craved pleasure, I couldn't hold back. I pulled up my gown, leaving only my shoulders covered. My hands caressed my skin, and with my fingertips, I aroused each inch of skin. I could sense my body coming out of its heedlessness. My breasts became tense, making my nipples hard. These were signs that gave away the pleasure I was succumbing to. It felt like a million tiny dancer ants were dancing within my womb. I could perceive the humidity of my arousal even without touching myself.

I instinctively spread my legs apart, leaving the amazing triangle of pleasure without any barriers. I quietly moan while I move my hips to an unheard rhythm. Later, I introduce my fingers into my vagina, exploring its soft and delicate walls. Then I press my wrist against my mons pubis and start, and I continue to rub them together. The fingers within me try to reach this very spot, almost as if I could reach it through the walls of my vagina. Touching this spot makes my excitement augment and become ten times more intense.

I touch a button that is capable of generating thousands of volts of stimuli in my breast and almost exploding my womb. I shiver with excitement and humidity rises, I touch this spot gently, and it demands to be touched again. I can't stop doing it. I am so stimulated I lose grip on myself and let go of instinct and desire. Hot flashes invade my delirious body. They make it impossible to breathe. I contract myself to the point my knees touch my breasts. The dam breaks, letting all my fluids loose, wetting my hands, thighs, and my ordinary bed sheet.

I lay there without being able to muster any strength to move. I experienced the three longest minutes in the universe. Shortly after I gained my tranquility back, I still breathed heavily until I began to calm myself. My wet hand shook like a leaf against the wind in a tempestuous storm.

After the morning mass and breakfast, Sister Blanca comes to my room. She was around 45 years old and a woman in the peak of life. She sat on my cot next to me and inquired about my ailing body. Nervously, I stuttered.

*"I hardly slept last night. I had nightmares and woke up indisposed. I added."*Maybe it's the reason I'm so debilitated and have a headache. She laid her delicate hands on my forehead, trying to palpate any sign of fever. From my lying position, I could sense her jasmine-infused aroma.

Her eyes danced over my body, but she would immediately close them to hide her arousal. You could still breathe the aroma of my pheromones in the room, as I still wore last night's gown; it had imprinted on it the smell of my fluids.

She caressed my face with tenderness, her fingers touched my skin, and without hesitating, I grabbed her hand and started kissing it while nibbling on her fingers.

"What are you doing, you senseless little girl?"

She asked me without moving.

I took her by her headdress and drew her close to me. I offered my lips while I reached for a kiss. She didn't resist. Sister Blanca offered me her quivering mouth filled with desire; we continued to kiss for a long time. Until she got up and locked the door, she went back to lay with me. She started to undress me while kissing my lips, face, and eyes. She took her headdress off and let her short blond hair loose.

Stripped of her long and puritanical habit, I discovered her beautiful body. Below her belly, she hid the mark of a past pregnancy. She stood in front of me while I was seated on the side of my cot; I drew her near and started tenderly kissing her abdomen. I reached for her vast and round breasts that always gave off the jasmine aroma. Later, I found out that it was because she hid these tiny flowers on her breasts under her garments.

My face lingered over the surface of her body, I breathed in her aroma, and my hands went over her back and behind. I could feel her bewilderment, and with delicacy, I let myself fall over my back. She placed herself over me, she kissed me again, and I breathed in the smell of mint from her mouth.

She fondled my breasts with her hands. I spread my legs apart, and she joined me, straddling me and rubbing her vagina over mine. This sensation felt wonderful and provoked an infinity of new pleasures. She didn't stop moving until our fluids poured down my anus, finally reaching my sheets.

I didn't stop myself. After that conquest, I seduced Sister Rita. I had no limits; I could share my bed with three women at a time. It was pure ecstasy. There was no way this could have had a happy ending.

One day, when I was enjoying Sister Blanca's caresses, Sister Rita showed up unexpectedly at my door, catching us in the middle of a heavy and passionate kiss. She was in the midst of pure shock, overtaken by rage and jealousy; she attacked fellow Sister Blanca, who was taken by surprise as she kissed my private parts.

She had no choice but to leave my room naked, completely terrified, through the halls of the convent while being chased by Sister Rita, who yelled obscenities at her.

All the other sisters and novices came out of their cells to see what the cause of such commotion was. This unpleasantly tragic but nevertheless amusing incident was fatal. Word of the scandal reached the mother and the priest. There was nothing we could do; our incident was the word of mouth of everyone in the convent. You could hear whispers relating our tragic ending in the convent's kitchen.

Both Sister Blanca and Sister Rita were removed and transferred to other convents. The Catholic hierarchy made them disappear, just as it has done with other scandals.

My punishment was different.

They locked me up in my cell, completely prohibiting me from leaving until my mother picked me up. When my mother arrived, she was informed of my conduct. She almost died in place due to the public shame I had caused her.

Needless to say, I was expelled from the convent due to my lewd and lascivious behavior. However, I had found my true sexual preferences. My life was forever marked by the events that led me to accept my sexual orientation. Nothing would make me change my preferences when it came to choosing who I would enjoy in bed.

While we traveled back home, my mother did not stop recriminating me the whole way back. Never before had someone crossed the entire Atlantic Ocean being subject to endless recrimination. The long return home, which in itself is a boring and monotonous trip, felt as though it would never end. My mother would try to control any movement I would make, any gesture or pity intent of fraternizing with women aboard.

When we finally reached America, I inhaled. I was back in my life. I don't think anyone has felt such intense joy as I did when I saw the Statue of Liberty. I was overtaken by pure happiness. To me, the statue was a beacon of my own independence. Like the rest of the passengers on board, mostly European immigrants, my eyes gleamed with the sight of a possible new life. I was a completely different woman from the one that had left New York a while back.

During the first months, I spent my time locked away inside my house. I could only leave accompanied by my own mother or brothers. I rebelled and threatened her that I would elope with the first person I could, whether man or woman; it didn't matter as long as I would be set free of her rigid and strict vigilance.

Slowly, she began to let loose and would slowly liberate me of her strict supervision. It started with a couple of parties here and there. Maybe she thought that I surely wasn't capable of repeating the incidents in France.

She was totally wrong. While in the convent, I had enjoyed a delicious and exquisite feast, making me entirely addicted to the pleasures of women. If I was to pay for my lascivious sins, I was thoroughly ready to pay for them.

But nothing would make me change my decision or stop me from enjoying the delicacies of a woman's naked body covered by my kisses and clothed with my desires.

Lovers of the New York Theaters were conquered by the gaze of a beautiful and mischievous Russian actress, *Alla Nazimova*, who had arrived in the Big City back in 1905 from London, where she had acquired considerable success. She established a Russian theater in the Lower East Side of Manhattan. Broadway would open up its door for her in 1906, paving her way to success with critics and the public.

Fate led us to each other unexpectedly. It was November 16th, 1916. Her film *"War Brides"* was premiering that night, and an old friend from home, who was especially fond of my sister Rita, had invited us.

Later, we would be part of the small soiree thrown in honor of the actors and production staff.

Alla Nazimova was 37 years old but was still stunning and amazingly good-looking. However, there was a sort of quirkiness to her beauty. Her big eyes were her weapon of choice when it came to seducing; her languid stare, which she laid carelessly over her shoulders in well-rehearsed poses, made her a quite alluring actress.

After the screenings, I lingered close to her while I listened to her captivating voice, which was accompanied by a strong Ukrainian accent. She would add to her allure by speaking certain words in French. Alla, quite the expert in the art of seduction, noticed my bewildered self. Fixing her intense gaze upon me, she questioned me about my doings there that night.

"Are you an actress, or do you dream of becoming one?"

I left little room between us and stared into her eyes while I whispered so no one else could hear me:

"I am no actress, but if you asked me to, I would become one just so I could always be this close to you and feel your gaze upon me."

I don't know if this baffled her, but she smiled without taking her eyes off me. A waiter happened to walk by; she called him and asked him for two glasses. She handed me one and smiled, nodding to the group of persons she was with as if asking permission to leave the room. Alla took me by the arm, leading me through the hall.

We reached a spacious fanlight, leaving behind us everything and everyone at the party. We gazed upon the half-lit garden in front of us. My mind couldn't stay in one place. I did not know what the consequences of my actions would be. Nevertheless, I didn't regret anything.

She spoke to me in a soft voice, and dragging her speech she said:

"Petite, vous voulez tenter le danger?"

"Oui madame, j'aime le danger et ses conséquences."

We went out to the terrace. The moon shone over the garden, while the cold weather made me shiver. Alla noticed, and smiling, she asked me.

"Are you cold, little one?"

"Yes, a bit."

"Would you like to come in? If you wish, I can warm you up in the arms."

"Warm me up? Do you really think you could manage to warm me up?"

I said in a provoking manner while maliciously smiling.

She chuckled while grabbing me by my waist and making me turn towards her. Without speaking a word, she kissed my lips. I let myself go inundated by the seduction of her eyes and lips. We kissed under the moonlight while her warm and moist tongue warmed the inside of my mouth. I laced my arms around her neck while she continued to grab my waist. Her embrace was so strong; her breasts hardly let me breathe.

"Do we leave this party?" She inquired in between kisses.

"Yes," I muttered while I kissed her neck.

We went around the garden until we reached her car; as soon as her chauffeur saw us, he opened the door and drove us to her home.

She lived in a magnificent residence on Park Avenue and 20th St. The maid received us. I was astonished by the decoration and the tapestry that hung on the wall that depicted great hunting scenes. I stayed close to the white marble chimney. We left the party so suddenly we had left our coats behind, and the cold weather made my bones ache. Alla came back to me, dressed in a sheer tunic, revealing her entire naked body. Her blushed face gave away the desire that was overtaking her, her eyes gleamed the way the fire did in the chimney. I was in awe and felt the desire run through my body.

"Do we toast to love and pleasure?"

She asked while she handed me a glass of wine.

"To love and pleasure."

I slowly took a sip of the wine and felt it go down my throat, heating my body up. We wouldn't take our eyes off each other. I let myself go while I inhaled the aroma of the wine I savored. The sweet and bitter taste of ripe grapes inundated my mouth, and suddenly, I felt a strange sensation on my back, a sort of electric current coming down from my neck to my coccyx, and it ended with a bursting and pleasant sensation on my rear.

She left the glass on the table, and so did I. Her arms once more surrounded my waist. I placed my hand on her face, and we kissed. One kiss, two kisses, three kisses, a long kiss, and the never-ending kiss…my body is heating up. My hands untied her tunic while it came down her body.

Her skin felt warm to my touch. I heard her moaning while my lips searched for her breasts. I tenderly kissed them and played with her hard nipples. She laid herself over her white carpet beside the fireplace. I kneeled over her lower abdomen, and the tip of my fingers and my lips ran all over her skin until I reached her labia, right between her thighs.

I breathed in her aroma. I played with her hair while I kissed her. I teased her until she became desperate. She would moan with pangs of emotion while she would call me "Mon Petit" and "Petit diable."

She grabbed hold of my hair with desperation; unsuccessfully, she would try to close her thighs before the eminent rupture of her spring. Every part of her body became hard while she moaned. She yelled in a language unfamiliar to me and suddenly grabbed hold of my face with her inner thighs to the point of suffocation. Her body came back to normal; her eyes started looking for mine, and a slight smile appeared on her face.

"Mon amour, ta bouche est magnifique," she said while looking to lock her lips with mine. We continued to see each other a couple of times. We shared our bed with plenty of women. I had entered a world I had never been a part of before. She opened the doors to a circle of very desirable women. I was unstoppable now; I had become part of this haute couture world of movie actresses. From her bed, I jumped straight into the bed of Tallulah Bankhead.

Tallulah was very young when I met her. She had recently moved to New York accompanied by her aunt Louise. Aunt Louise was her sort of chaperone since Tallulah was yet to turn 18. The baggage she brought with her came filled with dreams and aspirations to conquer Broadway. To star in a movie was her greatest dream, more than a dream, her biggest goal.

She was almost royalty, daughter, granddaughter, and great-granddaughter of famous southern democrat politicians of the era. She had reached small-town success in the theaters in Huntsville. Her extraordinary beauty was soon to open the doors of the film industry in Hollywood.

A couple of months after arriving in the Big City, she appeared in the movie "Who Loved Him Best?" That same year, she became a renowned actress by participating in "When Men Betray" and "Thirty a Week."

Days after turning 18, she set herself free of her aunt Louise's supervision and moved to the apartment of Bijou Martín, an actress who would soon become her demise.

Bijou introduced her to cocaine.

Tallulah would often say her father was a zealous Methodist man and spoke to her of the dangers men and alcohol would bring her. Before leaving for New York, Bijou had promised her father she would never try marijuana. A promise she always kept in exchange for not being bound by any other promise.

She wasn't a stranger to the love of women. We used to meet up frequently in the house of Alla. One day, she showed up with Bijou by her side. In these informal meetings, we talked about poetry, literature, and the success the actresses had.

Her beauty captivated me; I have always felt mesmerized by the beauty of blonde women. Maybe because they remind me of Cosette. I looked at her without missing a word that would come out of her mouth. Her blue eyes gleamed with freedom.

How could this be otherwise?

She had grown up in a well-off family and studied in a private school, very far away from the hardships most actresses on Broadway had endured.

How could she not be wild and free?

Ever since my time at the convent, I had discovered my skills as a seductive lover. I wasn't afraid of telling a woman how much I desired her. "There are no impossible women, only difficult women" became my motto.

And in the first opportunity I had, I whispered in her ear, "

You make my heart skip a beat. When you laugh, I feel I begin to lose control. When you caress me with your beautiful eyes, I sense I'm lost in you."

She stared at me while nervously biting her lips, which made her even more seductive. I held her left hand and delicately placed her over my breast, just above my pounding heart.

"See what you do to me?"

"You arouse my desire," she answered while unashamedly feeling my breasts.

"I would love to give in to your charm and savor the pleasures love could bring us. Would you like to join me?

Alla had disappeared with Bijou a long time ago. Besides, nothing tied me to them except the fact that we shared our bed with the same circle of friends.

"It will surely be a delightful night if I share it with you."

She continued to seductively bite and lick her lips while she maliciously fondled my breasts.

I took her by the hand and made her walk to the room I slept in when I didn't sleep with Alla. I closed the door behind her and pulled her close to me. I pushed her hair away from her face and stared into her blue eyes, provoking her desperation for my lips.

I breathed in her body's aroma while I held her tightly by her waist. She couldn't take it. She reached for my lips like someone gasping for air.

I had seen Isadora Duncan on stage many times.

I loved the way she danced. All you would hear were phrases like *"Isadora dances like a goddess."* She didn't dance. She flew on stage. The way she moved her arms, similar to the waves of the ocean, made her a unique dancer.

Her long hair moving around almost seemed like it became a part of her choreography. Her ethereal and sometimes sheer tunics revealed her gorgeous body. Her bare feet moved almost without touching the stage, and her clothes danced around like the waves of the ocean. Her dance presentations were indeed true works of art.

Coming out of a magnificent function, Isadora had fully displayed what made her such a great dancer. There were more than 20 of us, fully liberated women with no moral ties and with no men to spy on them. We were quite the bunch that night.

We took off in various cars from the theater on Broadway to her house in the Village.

There was music coming from an *"Edison Bell"* jukebox that played vinyl, such as *"Vesti la giubba"* by Enrico Caruso and *"A la luz de la luna"* by the Spanish duo Emilio de Gorgoza.

Our chatter rose in volume, and the glasses of wine and whiskey filled and emptied each minute. Isadora sat near a spacious sofa, contemplating us. We had exchanged words before when we ran into each other at a friend's house.

I felt admiration for her, and she attracted me as a woman. I knew her sexual preferences were aligned with mine. She had been with a couple of my friends. I got close to her and indulged in small talk. She asked me about my poems and literary endeavors.

She confessed to me just how much tired she was. Her feet were hurting to the point she could no longer stand. I offered to give her legs a massage, and she agreed and invited me to follow her into her room.

I took a small bottle of almond oil that was on her dresser. Just like I had offered, I began to massage her while she lay down. Kneeling on her bed with my hands soaked with oil, I grabbed her gorgeous and sculpted leg and began rubbing her and caressing her thighs.

With each stroke, my fingers became more defiant; I began rubbing her golden locks while she closed her eyes in a state of complete ecstasy. I went down her legs and massaged her delicate feminine feet. I couldn't get a hold of myself at that moment.

Lascivious thoughts permeated my mind. The image of her vagina infant of me lay like a delicious feast before my eyes. It was at that moment that I was determined that I would seduce her.

First, I poured oil on her feet and started rubbing them. Later, I traced her heels firmly with my fingers. There was a place on the sole of her foot that I knew regulated all sexual activity.

I had to get my hands off that point.

When I did, I felt how her body jumped under the effects of the electrical impulses sent by the erogenous point I stimulated. When she moaned, I knew I had her served on a platter.

I played with her fingers, stretching them delicately; I rubbed my fingers against hers. I could feel her purr like a kitten. She quivered on her bed like the sheets burned her back.

I went back to her thighs while still caressing her. I was done with the massage I was unto something else now. She half opened her eyes and looked at me, and I began rubbing against her…she was mine now.

She spread her legs open, inviting to dine with the feast between her legs. I took in her aroma as that of a female in heat. I went down on her, and with my mouth, I liberated open a dam of sweet nectar.

After her failed attempts to correct my behavior in the convent, my mother did not give up; she would do the impossible to make a *"fine lady"* out of me.

Her next plan was to set up an arranged marriage for me behind my back. Marriage was, for her, the only solution. Her first step was to find a suitable candidate among her inner circle of friends. Perhaps a man from our same social class and with dubious sexual preferences. She visited a painter's sisters, and with them, she managed to set up a wedding.

They set the date, and like that, they planned our lives without our consent. Their only concern was to avoid being the talk of everyone in town.

Abraham Poole was a recognized painter. He was good-looking and from a nice family. He was also homosexual.

It was the perfect arrangement to save both families. I had no choice but to accept. However, I was very clear that none of this would change my ways. Poole's sister and my mother had arranged everything behind our backs; we would also arrange something for them behind their backs.

We were both honest about our sexual preferences and accepted each other; we would live independent lives while living together.

The wedding was in 1920; I had just started my relationship with the actress Eva Le Gallienne. I loved her; we were really involved with each other, and my world revolved around her.

On the day of the wedding, I arrived with a gray dress. The guests stared at me, and I could sense their doubt. Somehow, this was my way of rebelling against a society that imposed their beliefs and ideas without any consideration of human dignity.

We never slept together. We never shared our bed. We never consummated our marriage. I never had sex with a man.

In the beginning, all I did was exchange kisses with a boy when I was really young. However, it never went further than teenage kisses and playfulness.

We divorced after 15 years.

At the end of 1920, I went with Eva to Constantinople. I was in the lobby of the hotel where we were staying when I first laid my eyes on Greta Garbo.

When I saw her, I was shocked. I felt an intense attraction to her goddess-like aura. I couldn't speak a word. I couldn't understand what was happening to me. Everything I felt was completely irrational, like a clue left in my destiny. Her face was forever etched on my mind; I began to look for her all over without any luck.

Shortly after our first encounter, we saw each other again on the street. I didn't get the chance to speak to her; I was too nervous to muster the strength to speak to her with confidence.

I didn't know who she was or what friends we had in common. *"Maybe she is part of the recently exiled Russian royalty,"* I thought.

One night, I managed to fight my fear and ask the receptionist if she could tell me more about Greta.

"A Swedish starlet," she said and added that she was the new up-and-coming star of the film world. When I saw her, I noticed the magnetism behind her beauty, her slow and sensual walk. Those were gestures and details that didn't go unnoticed by my expert eyes. She was like me, a woman in need of love from another woman.

My brothers were all very reserved and quiet, just like my father and his Cuban relatives, full of fears and forever preparing themselves for future crises. Never leaving behind a life of eccentricities like those left by the women I dated.

Our eldest sister was born in October of 1875, Rita de Acosta, better known by the rest of the world as Rita Lydig.

The press presented her as the *"most eccentric woman in America,"* famous for her extravagance and the elegance she inherited from her great aunt. Rita became a sculptor and philanthropist and founded the first eye bank in America.

Like her great-aunt, she became romantically involved with artists and painters. She was a model for Giovanni Bolding and John Singer Sergeant, photographed by Adolf de Myer, Edward Steichen, and Gertrude Käsebier. Malvinas Hoffman even sculpted an alabaster bust of her.

Rita wrote the novel *"Tragic Mansions"* in 1927, under the pen name of Miss Philip Lydia, a high society melodrama. The novel received acclaim from the New York Times, describing it as being *"emotional and appealing."*

Her most iconic and elegant outfits went on to become pieces in the Museum of Metropolitan Art.

Aida was born in July 1884. She was the wildest one of all of us, the bohemian one. One time, when she was 19 years old and strolling through the streets of Paris with my mother, she looked up in the sky and saw a zeppelin flying in the air. Her adrenaline shot up all over her body, and from that time on, she was determined to conquer the sky.

Alberto Santos-Dumont was the man flying the zeppelin; he would soon become her teacher and maybe even her lover, but no one is really sure. What is certain is that he always kept a picture of my sister on his desk and a vase full of fresh flowers next to it. Mr. Santos-Dumont flew almost every day. Aida looked for him, and a couple of friends in common introduced them to each other. Aida convinced him to teach her how to fly. Aida became the first female to fly a powered aircraft solo, six months before the Wright brothers.

After her many lessons, she flew in the small aircraft by herself. Santos and my sister went to see a polo match in Bagatelle, where the North American and British teams faced each other.

When the match was over, Aida asked Santos if she could fly the zeppelin by herself, and he couldn't find himself to say no to her. She flew all the way to Santiago de Neuilly while Santos guided her.

When they landed, Mr. Santos-Dumont asked her, *"How did you like it, miss?"*

To which she replied, *"It was quite pleasant, Mr. Santos-Dumont."*

He yelled in enthusiasm, *"Mademoiselle, you are the first woman to fly an aircraft like this!"*

She was always considered unique and special and was photographed and sculpted by the notable artists of the period. Aida lived in New York, Paris, and London. Among her friends, you could find remarkable figures such as Edgar Degas, Auguste Rodin, León Tolstoy, Sarah Bernhardt, Ethel Barrymore, and Claude Debussy.

John Singer Sergeant was famously quoted saying, "She is art in itself," about my sister.

In 1900, Aida received two million dollars after her divorce from William Earl Dodge Stokes. An almost unheard amount of money back in that time. She traveled to Europe and enjoyed staying at *the Ritz* with her posse, which included her hairstylist, chauffeur, and personal assistant.

She lived carelessly and was highly esteemed by the American, English, and French high society.

Just as it is with our family tradition, she died bankrupt.

"*These were years guided by the spirit of the New Era,*" "*We were close to the fire, with a passion to create and the courage to accomplish.*"

These were magic words, the phrases that inspired me and served me as a guide at the beginning of the 1920s.

While I lived in New York, I would often visit Harlem. These were seen as the slums of the city by the white and wealthy who went to Harlem for fun, sex, and illegal alcohol. Until 1920, a woman by herself in a bar could be considered a harlot. The law was very severe with women who visited bars by themselves. Harlem was the best place to escape from the rigid customs and traditions of New York's elite society.

There were many bars, theaters, cabarets, and restaurants you could choose from to break the famous ban on alcohol. It was custom to go out at six in the afternoon, go get dinner, and then leave for the theater and finish having breakfast with your party clothes the next day while everyone else was getting ready to start their day of work.

On January 26th, 1934, the theater *"Hurting and Seaman Burlesque"* would become the Apollo Theater, on 125th St in Upper Manhattan. This place would become the platform that shot many famous blacks to stardom, with four shows per night, seven days a week, plus 12 additional shows on Wednesdays, Saturdays, and Sundays. They added up to 31 shows per week.

This theater was nothing like any other theater.

I loved going to 42nd St and Lenox Ave. to the *"Cotton Club"* and feeling the musical notes coming from the big bands.

Being able to enjoy each one of those nights was a very special opportunity. The Cotton Club was the place where you would go during the prohibition. You could ask for a *"Chicken Cock"*, and they would bring you a bottle of whiskey inside a sealed tin can.

We enjoyed one of the most delightfully entertaining shows. We delighted ourselves with the music from the best black entertainers of the time, like Fletch Henderson, Coleman Hawkins, Don Redman, Dorothy Fields, and Kimmy McHugh. They were later followed by another generation of great composers: Ted Koehler, Harold Arlen, and The Cab Calloway band.

Coles Atkinson's dancers were always beautiful women dressed in small outfits. We listened to popularly acclaimed singers such as Adelaide Hill, Ethel Waters, best known by her artistic name *"Sweet Mama Stringbean,"* and Johnson Mayo. Harlem's nightlife was incredible.

Nevertheless, and without a doubt, the best club was the *"The Clam House"* on 133rd St., the most controversial club when it came to lesbian women of the time.

I loved going dressed in a pantsuit, with my hair slicked back with Vaseline, just like the hottest male stars of the time. I would accessorize with a stylish hat, and my custom-tailored shoes were embellished with buckles.

This famous bar was owned by the famous singer Gladys Bentley, who had turned this club into a very special place where she was the main star. She would go up on stage dressed in a white tuxedo and a top hat. What an amazing blues singer she was. Oh, and how she loved to sing songs with double meaning while flirting with the women in the audience. It was popular opinion that Gladys had gotten married in Atlantic City to a white woman and that they lived together in New Jersey.

It was the hottest club for women like us, Amazonians on a faraway island just for women, and some few scatter men of dubious sexual orientation.

We were comfortable being ourselves there; it was our home away from home for many women from the upper and middle class of the city and many out-of-state visitors in search of adventures.

After hours of drinking alcohol and smoking marijuana, it was normal to see couples dancing, embracing each other to the rhythm of the music, or even finding couples in the shadows or in the restrooms in the middle of a heated public display of affection.

The place was perfect for brewing intense passions and letting loose into complete debauchery. You could go by yourself, with a lover, or with multiple lovers. We were all nameless lovers there, women who loved white and black women; this was our sacred Lesbos Islands, and we were vestal virgins.

Black women had different customs than we did. Most of the ones we met at the club were truly bisexual and were even married. Some even had husbands who knew what they were doing. It was a crazy world.

It was an unforgettable night for me, the time I had the opportunity of having two black women one night. I was quite drunk. There is no denying it.

Both of them were dancers at the club who had permission to mingle with the public. Some even prostituted themselves to the wealthy clientele. I saw one walk by my table. I had never been attracted to a black woman before, and my favorites have always been blondes. But something about her caught my eye.

Maybe it was her caramel-colored skin or her lips, maybe the firmness of her body or her tight bottom put on display by her skimpy outfit. I saw her walk by, and she noticed me staring, inviting her to walk past my table again.

I called her, and she came to the table I shared with my friends. She carefully looked at me and each one of my mates. Maybe she feared one of them was my lover. I moved a chair very close to me, and since I was wearing a suit, it was very easy for me to seat her almost between my legs.

"Are you looking for something?" I asked her while whispering on her neck.

"Yes, I'm looking for someone who can keep me awake all night."

"So, you like action?"

"Yeah, I need some action tonight; I need it. Can you give it to me?"

"You are a very naughty girl, I see. You like to provoke, but you also like the challenge. I will make you spend a night you won't forget."

She smiled provokingly.

"You really think so? It can be the other way around. Have you really had the chance to look at me? There is a lot of fire and passion inside of me."

She commented while she let me see the curves of her body. This image aroused me. The heat invaded my body, my mouth salivated, and other parts of my body became moist.

"Do we leave?"

I said while breathing in her natural scent, the smell of a woman ready to turn herself into desire. She didn't speak a word. She took me by my waist and just left with me. I knew a hotel that we used to frequent in case our passions didn't give us enough time to go back to our houses in New York. We were about to take a cab when a gorgeous woman came in between us.

"Take me, too, and you will be the queen of tonight. You will get to know your two servants, and you will be catered to by your two slaves," she offered.

I hesitated, but only for a few seconds. It was too much temptation for someone like me. I had never had two black women at the same time. The thought of it had intrigued me. And that night, the opportunity presented itself.

I saw my girl, and I liked how aggressive she was. I knew they both would try to outdo one another.

"Yes, let's go," I said while I motioned for her to go in the cab.

It was a small and discreet hotel with spacious and clean beds. Most importantly, staff members saw nobody, nor did they hear anything, no questions asked or indiscreet looks. We were visitors with no name or address, clients that would only stay for one night. A Mr. or Ms. Smith as long as we paid ahead for the room and a contraband bottle of whiskey.

After getting to our room, I went inside to the bathroom. When I came out, the whiskey bottle was already opened. The girls had already started on the bed. I liked how their beautiful lips interlocked with an exquisite sensuality. They were undressing one another. Their tongues savored the other's supple skin. They moaned like defenseless kittens. I opted to become a passive spectator. I took my clothes off, taking in the image present before me while I drank my whisky.

Naked on my bed, their ebony skin glowed against the white sheets. I was bewitched by their firm and black bodies, their breasts, and black nipples that looked like black pearls ready to be tasted.

The sensual girls gave themselves up to their pleasure without restraint. With their moist tongues, they tasted each part of their bodies in an indescribable 69. The room became inundated with the smell of their pheromones. A sweet aroma bloomed in the air while I touched myself, and I became completely moist with the streams from my spring. I arched my back from the intense pleasure I had given myself. I was barely regaining my breath when they both came for me and took me to the bed, where they had just been enjoying themselves.

"Ready to be served like Hippolyta, the Amazonia queen loved by Ulysses in the Iliad?" asked the first one.

"Will you let yourself be loved by both of us?"

"I am ready," I whispered without any idea of what I would face next.

They tied my extremities to the bedposts. Each girl began her share of love. While one kissed me, the other one ran her lips over my neck. They took turns to make love to me.

A thousand sensations ran through my body. I moaned and arched my body in intense pleasure. It was so much; I lost count of how many times I came. It was one after the other. When I thought I could no longer wet myself, I ended up in the mouth of one girl while the other intensely licked my foot.

My heart was beating fast, and my temples–so I thought–would burst while I came. I was left with no strength; I had to gasp for air from time to time, and sweat was dripping off my entire body. Little by little, my blood pressure came back to normal. I was completely exhausted, and completely disregarding my state, they started devouring themselves.

It was an incredible experience; I had come to understand how lavish the caressing of two African American women can be if their mind is up to making you their queen, ruler of a night full of pleasure. They turned out to be great lovers and mates.

I continued to live in New York City in this unfiltered and crazy debauchery when, one day, I received a job offer from Hollywood to work as a production assistant and as a screenwriter!

I might be remembered as a successful designer, writer, screenwriter, or Latin American poet. I especially wrote for Eva Le Gallienne, my lover, for almost five years. We worked together on two plays, *"Sandro Botticelli"* and *"Johanne d'Arc."*

Eva Le Gallienne abandoned me for Alice De Lamar, a wealthy patron of the arts. Alice was disappointed by the sales commercial theater was having, and with the economic sponsorship of her lover, a rich Colorado gold mine heiress who later went on to become the founder of the *"Civic Repertory Theater"* in New York. Her sponsorship was decisive for the success of theater in the United States.

I put all of my solitude and pain into rescuing the old and forgotten work I had stored in my drawer. It was a play I had started years ago about anti-semitism in a small town in New England. It debuted on Broadway in 1927. The reviews were very favorable, and an important critic wrote: *"Perfectly merged, perfect acting, and directed perfectly."*

The New York Times called it a *"well-written play, a solid work"*. In total, I wrote a dozen plays, two musicals, three poetry volumes, two novels, and two movie scripts, but as it turns out, close to the end of my life, I think that no one remembers any of my work.

"You can't dismiss Mercedes so easily. She has had two of the most important women in the U.S.: Greta Garbo and Marlene Dietrich."

–Alice B Toklas, in a private letter to his friend Anita Loos.

I lived my life to the fullest; I loved and was loved, and however, there was one that never fully responded to the intensity of my love for her. She was the most beautiful of my lovers, the most desired by men and women. She was known as *"The Diva,"* *"The Goddess,"* and "The Ice Princess,*"* but I always called her "The woman *I loved the most."*

She was Greta Garbo.

I loved her figure and rendered tribute to her Scandinavian goddess halo. I kissed the ground she walked upon; I built an altar where I worshipped her. Nevertheless, she only regarded me as a tool to satisfy her lustful pleasures, her cravings, and her abuse. I got to know her so well that I even knew about the hatred she felt towards the social class she came from.

All of her different aspects were real; everything about her personality was genuine and something I had not seen in anyone before.

Nonetheless, she could easily turn into the most loving being or hateful being, becoming a victim of radical mood swings most of her life. Even in school, her oscillating personality would show through, and later on stage, she would obsessively rehearse scenes until she became satisfied with the result. It was typical of Greta to push everyone out of the room, leaving her and the cameramen alone to perfect her acting.

I never knew another lover like her; a thin and frail woman of 5'7" who barely weighed 127 pounds, within her laid the force of her Viking heritage. She was the personification of the goddess Freyja.

In Eddas, Freyja is described as the goddess of love, beauty, and fertility. People worshipped her in hopes of obtaining success in love, giving birth, and for prosperous seasons. Freyja was also a deity associated with war, death, magic, prophecy, and wealth. It also goes on to mention that in her palace, she received the wounded in battle.

That was Greta; she gave you all her love while caring for your wounds just for the pleasure of watching you lose yourself while making love to her.

Her strong and raspy voice did not exude femininity when mad but was exceedingly sensual when she loved. There were days when I felt raped during intense sessions of pleasure she put me through, and there were other days where her period made her stay away from our bed. During those days, she would turn into a cold Scandinavian peasant, a complete stranger to smiles or words of affection.

It was characteristic of her to go from the most intense moments of pleasure to the least; she oscillated between inextinguishable lusts to total apathy. I suspected the root for this lay in her existential fears. Greta lived in constant fear of someone revealing her homosexuality.

Discretion and loyalty were her golden rules. Whoever broke them fell into complete oblivion for Greta. That's what happened to Marlene Dietrich, who treated Garbo like another conquest after becoming involved during the production of a movie in 1925. They pretended not to know each other, almost ignoring each other's existence until 1945, when Orson Welles introduced them to each other.

Her fear of aging in front of the public eye was colossal, to say the least. She did not wish to experience her beautiful image aging in front of the camera. Another fear imposed itself on her life: the fear of her homosexuality becoming public. She refused to become the latest gossip.

Little by little, she revealed more about her life to me. Greta started smoking when she was a little girl; the reason why she started dressing like a boy was because she felt comfortable and confident.

"I feel like a solitary man wondering about on earth," she would say.

Her first lesbian experience was with her sister Alva at a campsite. On one summer night, they played Mom and Dad. Many times before, they had seen their parents have sex, all because her dad was an alcoholic who had sex with her mom without any regard for the little kids who were also in the room. She was barely 14 years old.

They kissed and caressed each other, fueled by the curiosity of the game more than any sentiment regarding lust.

Shortly after, Eva Blomgren, a girl a couple of years older than her, would introduce her to many pleasures Greta did not know before. Opened a world of new experiences for men and women. They would always go to exotic islands with Eva and her friend Gustav. The three of them would indulge in orgies. This was a defining experience for her. Greta would rather wait for Eva than have a taste of the boring young Gustav.

In the Royal School of Acting, she met Mimi Pollack, a girl two years younger than her. She made Greta completely lose her emotional stability. During rehearsals, *Mimosa*, as she would call her in intimacy, would always be by her side. Garbo was never as sweet or caring as she had been with Mimi. Garbo loved her with the passion fueled by her adolescence and with the innate good sense of her blooming maturity.

A letter she wrote in 1924 divulges how her relationship with Mimi led her to be a victim of her own destructive jealousy: *"You have stirred up a storm inside of me," "Think of me and remember time flies by, and I could be arriving at your house soon, and when I do, I don't want to have gray hair, all because of your infidelity."* When Garbo found out about her marriage, she wrote her a long letter where she inquired: *"I dream about seeing you and asking if you still believe in you old lover."*

She would finish the letter with an endearing *"Love you, Mimosa."* In 1926, when she heard about her pregnancy, she wrote: *"We can't help nature that way God intended, but I always assumed you and I would remain together."* She went to the extreme of believing she could be the father of Mimi's baby.

When Garbo heard about the birth of her child, she could not hide her joy and sent Mimi a telegram, where she excitedly exclaimed: *"I feel incredibly proud of being the father."*

In 1929, she went back to Stockholm just to spend an entire season close to Mimi. I feel as though I suffered an incredible loss because she never loved me with the same intensity she loved Mimi. However, with time, it became apparent to me that the love she felt was based on this ideal concept of platonic love.

If destiny had not distanced them due to their contracts with MGM, she surely would have grown accustomed to Mimi and would have opted out of leaving her after a while. Greta loved her because she was distant and impossible. She regarded Mimi as the only viable option to focus all of her love on. Without a doubt, the change Mimi left in her when she decided to marry and have a family broke something within Greta. It made her feel less invincible. She distanced herself even more from men and from the thought of marrying against her will just to please society.

There was a phrase she once uttered, and it would become iconic to her: *"I will probably be alone the rest of my life; the word 'wife' is a bad word in my vocabulary."*

Maybe this was what motivated her to leave the actor John Gilbert at the altar in 1927. He was the only man who she casually dated for periods of her life. Gilbert and the director Leopold Stokowski were both publicly recognized lovers in her life. All others were flings or studio gossip. Most were impossible to validate or confirm.

"It saddened me deeply leaving Constantinople without a word, but sometimes destiny is much kinder than what we think, or maybe it's that we can't escape our destiny."

I wrote in my diary while the boat I was in left the shore in Constantinople headed for America in 1920.

I had just moved to Hollywood as a screenwriter and production assistant. Shortly after, and as karma repeating itself, I found her again.

I say again because I'm sure that in past lives we were lovers. Since our casual encounter in Constantinople, I had not seen her. She had continued to embark on her actress-on-the-rise career. I followed any news about her; there was no single article in newspapers or magazines that I did not avidly read. I did not miss a single one of her movie screenings, always with the illusion of being able to run into her even though I knew she did not attend her movie premiers.

We had a party at a writer's house, Selka Viertel, with whom I was involved in a fleeting romance. When Greta arrived, she illuminated the entire house with a golden glow. I was not expecting to see her, much less in this particular place.

At last, I was face to face with her again. Selka walked in her direction to welcome her, and I approached both of them. Innocently, I didn't think of the consequences this would bring for the three of us. Selka introduced Garbo to me, and I felt imprisoned, and an electrifying sensation traveled through my body. When it came time to stretch her hand, in that instant, like an old projection, memories of distant and aged memories flashed through my eyes.

I knew it somehow. Karma had to reunite us. I was embezzled by her beauty and manners once again. A twenty-six-year-old goddess that had just descended from the Olympus. I lost track and notion of every aspect of life in that instant.

Did we speak to each other?

Not really, she spoke, and I listened. She complimented my expensive bracelet that had been a gift from my own mother.

Once again, without any regard for consequences, I took off my bracelet and handed her the piece of jewelry. I immediately lied:

"Since I saw you for the first time in Constantinople, I have been consulate thinking about you. I bought this bracelet in Berlin while thinking about you. Please wear it as a sign of my devotion and love towards you."

I stared at her big smile, and for a while, I believed she had been genuinely moved. However, affection and submission were ordinary for her. She was used to these types of gifts.

If, in that same moment, she had asked for my beating heart and life, I would have given them to her for just a moment of her love, kisses, seductive eyes, blonde her, and lips that were created for the most exquisite kisses of tireless lovers. Those lips were hardly ever the outline of smiles, but they surely knew how to arouse lust and desire in others. I was left without any strength, ideas, or thoughts. I was completely lost. The confident and seductive woman I once was caving into the astounding Swedish beauty in my eyes.

The second time we saw each other, she gave me a flower, and I felt the happiest of all women. I still keep it, just inside my bible, in which the covers are filled with pictures of her. I still keep it on my night table.

"Please forgive me, God, if I have offended you by placing pictures of her in the bible, but to me, Greta and you are my guides."

That flower is dried and withered like my heart, but it does not matter; I keep it like I would the most valuable object!

The second encounter did not happen by chance; in a moment of bravery, I called her. Selka had Greta's personal phone number written down in her phonebook. On more than one occasion, I lay on my bed with the number in my hands and the phone on my bed.

But one day, I just called her.

The fear crippled me and rendered me mute, so I hung up. I tried once more, and the sweet voice of the operator woke me up from my trance and asked me to which number I decided to speak. I was lying on my bed; it was close to ten o'clock when I answered the operator:

"Yes, I would like to speak with the number 1269. Would you put me through?"

"I will be glad to."

A moment later, another voice was on the other end of the line.

"Yes, Greta, good night, it's Mercedes De Acosta speaking to you. Please excuse my impertinence. I have been thinking about calling you for days and had not mustered the courage until today. You may hang up if you wish, and I won't bother you again. But I really wished to hear your voice and speak to you."

I said without taking a breath. All I heard was silence. Later, I perceived how she relaxed as she was talking to me.

"No, no, please do not hang up. If you called me, why not talk? Please tell me what it is that you wish."

I took a deep breath. I had begun to feel the lack of oxygen. I lay on my bed shaking like a vibrating guitar string struck by a songwriter.

"I wanted to chat with you, hear you, get to know you, and for you to get to know me better. I want you to realize how much I suffer for you, how I wish to be your slave like I was in our past lives. How I always will be your slave as long as I exist on this earth. We will run into each other today and tomorrow for one simple reason: Your life is forever linked to mine."

"How sweet are your words, my little one? All the love you have for me certainly touched me deeply. Are you sure of everything you profess?"

"Yes, I am more than sure of each one of the words I spoke. I know I have been your slave before, your toy, I know, and I just wish to continue being so. There's no other thing I want more."

"Would you like us to see each other? We could see each other one of these days and have coffee. Would you like that?"

"Of course! That is my greatest desire. Just set the day and time, and I will be

there to surrender myself to you.”

"Hahaha, you do know we will meet strictly for coffee, right? I would just like you to tell me those sweet phrases face to face. Does the day after tomorrow sound good for you? Yes? I will call you so we can set up where we will meet.”

Just like she had promised, she called me and said she would pick me up at my apartment in an hour. I ran desperately from place to place, trying to be as ready as I could be. I could not get a hold of myself. My hands were sweaty and would not stop shaking. I was ready to wait for her when she pulled up in her car in front of my building. I ran to meet her. I couldn't hide my nerves. I got in and took a seat next to her. I looked at her, completely marveling at her beauty. I could not take my eyes away from her. She took a rose from the seat, she took a napkin to her lips, kissing it, and then she gave it to me. As she gave it to me, I almost immediately placed my lips on the same spot she had kissed it.

She drove quietly around the city, looking for the nearest route to Santa Monica.

The entire way there, we kept silent, only interrupted by sporadic conversations. We set out to our destination. Once we got to the beach, she looked for an area close to the southern Spanish city. She parked the car away from the noise from the Pacific Ocean Park and the Santa Monica Pier.

We got out of the car and walked towards the beach, feeling the warm sand underneath our bare feet. We strolled close to the shore and enjoyed the tranquility. Around us were only anonymous couples enjoying the beach like us. I got infinite happiness from her company. I watched her contemplate how the horizon cast her shadow upon the shore. The sun appeared to look for her golden locks to create a beautiful halo around her face.

After walking for a while, we sat on the shore as the immense solar disc hid on the far horizon, coloring the ocean surface with fire-like tones and marking a pathway that invited us to a different dimension, to a place exclusively for the two of us. Her golden locks danced around in the wind, and her eyes reached a fiery tone that gave away the burning passion within her.

Silence wrapped us both.

All we could hear were the sounds of waves and, here and there, seagulls looking for their last prey of the day before going back to the nest. While she quietly observed the horizon, I continued to be captivated by her presence without taking my eyes off her. She came back to herself, turned her face towards me, and looked around to search for innocent bystanders who might witness our secret affair. But she did not see anyone else, so she gave me a small kiss.

A small kiss where our lips met for a couple of seconds, a kiss that seemed eternal, and where Freyja the goddess returned to earth, awarding me with her divine grace. She blushed while she regained her composure. I followed her movements, and just as she did, I looked around to see if anyone was around. I grabbed her by the waist, and I kissed her with all the passion I had carried within me since I met her in Constantinople. It was a kiss that carried all of my love, all of my desire, and I swear, I thought I would die with her body between my arms. The taste of her saliva made me lose all sense of time and space. We went back to Hollywood; I could still feel my lips swollen from the kiss. I kept savoring them with my tongue, trying to retain the taste of her lips.

Later, I whispered to her, *"Lady, I spent the afternoon by your side. Will you allow me to kiss your lips and feel the scent of your skin? Will you gift me with the joy of spending an entire day with you? Do it out of charity, I do not care, but let's getaway, just the two of us, far from curious stares. Will you let me love you like I desire?"*

"My little one, you are one intense woman and very demanding. Do you really think I would allow you inside my room?"

"That is my biggest ambition, to be able to go beyond the door of your room. I would do it without any hesitation."

"Do you really want it so badly?"

"Yes," I confessed immediately. "I really want it; I have been craving for this moment for years. Ever since our encounter in 1920, I have dreamt of the wonderful day when I would meet you again and you would grant me the opportunity of spending my life, love, and gestures with you."

"We will. I like your presence and determination and the force behind your words. We will. I will share my bed with you; we will go someplace where we will be by ourselves. No one will bother us."

When she left me at my door, we had already planned our escape. A couple of days later, we left for the Plata Lake in Nevada for six weeks.

I left Selka without saying a word, without writing her a note; I disappeared from her life, leaving behind a seed of hate and revenge in her heart.

La Plata was the perfect paradise for a wonderful discovery; it exceeded my expectations in every way. I fell to Greta's feet like many women before me. We lived an intense and tempestuous relationship for six weeks.

Her fear of being discovered made us get two different rooms right next to each other. After accommodating our luggage, we went for a walk around the lake.

The evening started to turn into a night, and my heart started to beat faster as each minute went by. But it seemed that she enjoyed making me wait for the moment I was craving.

A couple of hours had gone by since we had dinner; we were seated at the lake shore in front of our hotel. We spent more than two hours chatting while we shared a cigarette and drank wine. I could feel the coolness of the night breeze.

I looked at her and thought about kissing her and having her between my arms. She finally invited me to bed, and I rushed to follow her while a hot flash ran through my body.

I went inside my room to dress and clean myself up. I did not know what to wear to such an important encounter. I could not find anything feminine to wear. On the contrary, back home during the winter, I was accustomed to wearing male pajamas or being naked.

I sprayed perfume on my body. I wasn't sure if I should go out in male pajamas or in my birthday suit.

In the end, I decided to cover myself with a shawl and go to her. She was wearing a robe over her body and had dimmed the lights of the room by placing a scarf over the night lamp. Two glasses of wine awaited me; she smiled when she saw me.

"Come here, my little boy. I thought you would not come, and I would sleep alone."

Shaking, I approached her while she handed me a glass. I took it in my hands without taking my eyes off of her, for they shined like never before. The lighting in the room gave her blue eyes a golden sparkle, like a wild animal ready to have her prey.

"Let's make a toast to love, to this night, and those to come," she said.

"To love, to our love, to how lucky I am for spending the night with you, my goddess Freyja," I answered while we made the toast.

I drank up till the last drop of wine, and now she could not take her eyes off of me. When she finished her glass, she took mine and placed them on the night table. She took her hands to my face and placed her lips to mine. Without really kissing me, she grazed her lips on mine. Her hands kept me distanced from her while my hands were strongly clenched to her waist.

Finally, we kissed. First, it was a soft and tender kiss, but it swiftly changed to become a passionate interlock. We kissed in wild abandon. Our tongues savored each other. A while ago, I was in my shawl. Now, I was completely naked and at her full disposition. I was completely vulnerable and ready for her command. Without putting up resistance, I let her get her way with me.

Her mouth searched the skin over my neck, and I felt her cool tongue licking my neck. Her hands over my breasts followed the rhythm of her mouth, doubling my excitement. My legs began experiencing tremors; I could not hold myself together. She noticed my weakness, and without stopping her kisses, she took me to bed.

She laid me down and kissed every inch of my body. She started the route of savoring my breasts, my abdomen, my thighs. His tongue was the biggest of the sexual stimuli known to me until today. She turned me around, and now her mouth discovered new territory: my back.

I was lost in ecstasy. She spread my legs open, and I could feel the warmth of her breath over my bottom. She was looking for my nectar, and I gave it to her. I began to experience intense pleasure.

It was a piercing type of pleasure; it left me totally exhausted, and when I thought I could not go on anymore, she grabbed me once more. She would not stop. Her mouth savored my breast while her skillful fingers had their way with my clitoris. I was under a wild spell. I had no strength left in me to resist; I was ready to come once more, and when I did, all I could do was clench to her hand and try to stop the piercing pleasure. I grabbed her mouth and brought it to mine. I kissed her, and I bit her. I had to devour her lips and suck on them. It felt like the only way to make her mine. My back was warm, and I had dampened the sheet with my sweat. My cum left my thighs wet.

I took a deep breath while my sanity returned to me. She was straddling me, and I would not stop smiling. Her eyes gleamed with the satisfaction of knowing I had fallen prey to her skills as a lover. She remained lying together in a warmer embrace as she gave me a kiss. We kissed over and over again, and I felt a warm rush over me. Her lips were on my breasts again, but this time, she was nibbling on them. She loved how my tanned skin and dark aureoles contrasted against the white sheets. She went down on me.

She licked my pubis and played with my abundant black and curly hair. Her mouth was on my genitalia, and the piercing pleasure was back. I could feel how she devoured my genitalia with an inextinguishable appetite for her. She ate me up, and I let myself go in full pleasure. I moaned until I could not go on. We kissed passionately. Her mouth was full of my taste. I felt so lucky.

Queen Eddas, the Swedish princess, had made me feel the most intense pleasure possible. I had sex with many women before, but nothing could compare with what I had felt tonight. I felt I could float in heaven, that I could travel to Fólkvangr, her dwelling, in the beautiful Sessrúmnir. I could see her reign while I was her favorite slave.

We spent the night in complete debauchery and sex. Before dawn, she made a return to my room. That's how we kept appearances. She was always like this, completely obsessive about her image and hiding her sexuality. It seemed like her love for women made her vulnerable, like a sort of weakness that could ruin her femme fatale image fabricated by the Hollywood industry.

I will never forget the weeks we spent together. I never experienced those encounters ever again. She had fooled me. I thought she loved me. I thought I had conquered her heart.

We went out daily, sometimes in her car, and other times, we took long walks in the forest by the lake. Sometimes, we stopped in a secluded place, far from indiscreet stares. We had long talks about her life, her poverty-stricken childhood, the calamities her family had gone through, how she wasn't able to finish school, and how her lack of education left her feeling handicapped in the tough Hollywood industry.

La Plata Lake became home. In six weeks, I got to know the real Greta: completely irritable and short-tempered when her uterus cried for the need to be impregnated, joyful when the day turned out to fulfill her desires, unruly as a lover, and beaming with smiles if you could call that a smile, to the transformation of her face in some happy moments.

reta's mother left the countryside for a better life in the city, and what she found was an uneducated, alcoholic man who worked cleaning toilets. He was abusive and constantly hit her mother.

Even after all those years, those memories made her cry. She remembered how her mother sent her out every night to look for her drunk father, who preferred to stay in the tavern than go back home with his family.

With a stern face, she confessed to me how the day before he died, she found him lying on the street close to their house, completely drunk. She had to carry him all the way home, going up the stairs to their humble apartment. This image was a contrast with the loving father she remembered, the one who bought her gifts despite living in poverty. The father would buy her magazines and photographs of her favorite actors, all to incentivize her love for acting. She loved him despite the hurt he had caused her family.

Geza Von Cziffra, the movie director, happened to go into Greta's room by mistake, thinking it was director Stiller's room. Right when he went in, Greta was stepping out of the bathroom completely naked. He had the luck to appreciate her naked body. But he could not appreciate the work of art before him and decided to boast about the event in a callous manner:

"After seeing her in the story of Gösta Berling, where her face amazed me, I can say her full body did not even go on to cause me a favorable impression. No offense, but she looked like a green beanstalk with saggy breasts."

Those were his words among his inner circles. I can't share his opinion about her body, which was always perfumed with the scent of her favorite flower, violet.

You would never find her house adorned without this flower.

She was a very thin woman. When I had my arms around her, I could feel her bone structure just beneath her skin. Without a doubt, her face was the most beautiful one I had ever seen. Her languid blue eyes, her lost stare, always searching for a place far away, but very demanding when it came to searching for your attention. Her golden straight hair, each strand seemed to be made out of gold when the wind blew over them and the sun was upon them. Her oval-shaped face was the perfect shape, and her strong jaw accentuated the determination in words you would rather not hear in such a perfectly structured face like hers.

Her small and frail fingers, *Oh goodness!*

I must have kissed them a thousand times!

There were occasions when we slept together. I held her hands and placed them on my lips, and there I lay like worshipping a virgin.

Her small breasts were the size of a champagne glass. Her rose-colored aureoles contrasted against her white breasts. Her nipples were always hard, no matter the temperature. Her breasts seemed to have endured some strain.

They were not firm, like you would expect from a women who had not bore any children. We can't forget that the movie director, Stiller, made her lose over 30 pounds, which left some marks on her body. Her hips stood out even more than her thighs. Her ample hips made her one of the most desired women. Her perfectly sculpted legs, just in the right proportion to her torso, made her walk slower than usual to conceal the size of her feet.

Her feet were size 10, but their shape was perfect. Her small, rounded bottom tied her imperfect beauty together. Her genitalia were my favorite part. Her pubic hair was like the strands of hair you would find in a young corn kernel. Her copper scent was reminiscent of a mine, and her fluid was exquisite. The size was amazing due to the size of her thick labia and clitoris.

This often made her feel ashamed when she had sex with men because they did not understand just how big a throbbing clitoris could become when fully excited. Her genitalia were a heaven-sent gift for me. Having it in my mouth and having crazy orgasms made me afraid I would lose my head over her.

She was the perfect and wild lover I had waited for my entire life. She was the most desired woman by anyone. Full of wildness, audacity, fire, vehemence, delicacy, subtlety, and a complete expert in loving women, a skillful master in search of new ways to invoke pleasure. She made me the happiest woman on earth, right on her bed.

I had loved many women before, where I was always the dominant figure, but for her, I was her lady. In homosexual relationships, there is someone who plays the feminine counterpart. I was used to not being it. But with her, I had no option. Ever since we kissed near the Santa Monica Pier, I had no doubt she would be the dominant one. I would be her woman, and to me, she would be my everything.

She was the calm, full-of-composure lover who would not give in to emotional manifestations of any kind. Greta was incredibly stubborn and would refuse to make any emotional amends. This explained her fear of marriage, of revealing her sexual preferences, and her decision to disappear for long periods of time for internal healing, leading her to become very obsessive in relationships.

We went back to reality. We were back in Hollywood; she remained in her Santa Monica apartment close to the beach. Her life went back to rehearsals and work routine, almost as a way to hide herself from everyone. Her attires seemed to want to accomplish the same thing, with dark and ample sunshades and scarves around her head.

Each rehearsal and filming scene were all the same and had fallen into a routine. Making her life dull. At 8:30 in the morning, her car pulled up at the entrance of the studios to start her filming agenda. No other actor had arrived as prepared as her; she knew her lines by heart and did not waste time on rehearsals. Everyone on set knew just how demanding she was on herself, so barely anyone got in her way. At 5:30, her car would once again pull up to the entrance, marking the end of her filming. Her routine was so exact that it became a reference for anyone who wanted to adjust their watch. No matter the importance of the scene being shot, without a word, she would leave and return to her safe haven far from anyone and where no one could go in if he wasn't welcomed.

On numerous occasions, I visited her apartment, not every day, but just when she wanted to see me. I waited each afternoon for my phone to ring. I ran to pick it up and heard her soothing voice. That is what I always looked forward to.

"Maybe tomorrow we will see each other, my little girl."

She would finish the conversation while I was immersed in anguish and anxiety. I loved seeing her and spending time with her, talking and drinking, not too much, but just enough to make the evening more pleasant. I craved that closeness where we would spend nights awake undisturbed by any sounds but those of our talks and sporadic kisses.

When days went by without her calls, I started to be submerged in a depression. Nothing would cheer me up, not even casual encounters with other women that I had longed for before meeting Greta. Her anguish was contagious, and now I was a victim and part of her desolate existence.

In Hollywood, you could not find the distinguished places you could find in New York, so that limited our outings a bit. All you had was the Sunset Strip, with very glamorous bars where you could find the best music of the time. *"Ciro's," "Mocambo,"* and *"Trocadero"* were the places for the rich and famous. But they were missing the boldness and complicity you found in Harlem.

Some days, we took aquatic taxis from Venice Beach or from Ocean Park to the Boat Casinos three miles from the shore. We visited the *SS Tango* and the *SS Rex*, which was owned by the mobster Tony Carnero. You could freely gamble and drink far from any law to regulate alcoholic consumption.

The cabaret was a fantastic complement to our evenings. We would often go back to the shore accompanied by beautiful dancers who came from all parts of the US looking to become famous actresses in Hollywood. Our inner circle, comprised of people from the film industry, was very wary of indiscretion. We would meet with just a handful of friends, and if we decided to visit public places, we would go to bars like *"Big House"* or *"Lakeshore Bar,"* a place frequently visited by common day lesbians. The most expensive and elegant were the property of gangsters and mafia men like Mickey Cohen, a cold-blooded killer, son of a Ukrainian Jewish woman, born in Brownsville in Brooklyn, New York. He was a mid-level professional boxer, but his association with Frank Sinatra, Sammy Davis Jr., and the famous media mogul William Randolph Hearst had helped him to conceal his shady life.

The showbiz world is never too far away from criminal organizations like the mafia. The dividing line between Hollywood and the Mafia is always barely distinguishable. Needless to say, there were a few good places to have fun in Hollywood, but they did not compare to New York.

Movie stars were very affected by certain scandals, among them the biggest one of them all, the Arbuckle Scandal, which set the alarm for studio executives.

The big production companies started introducing *"moral clauses"* in their contracts with artists, which warned of annulling the contract if the artist's private life affected his public life negatively.

Many young ladies would enter Hollywood full of illusions; they thought they were headed for a new Babylon, but they really headed for a new Sodom and Gomorra. They would end up coming to face with eminent failure and being seduced into orgies organized by famous artists and made to work in brothels.

At the start, fairytale-like parties were organized, with numerous pretty women in search of a break or opportunity, but instead, they ended up in the hands of unscrupulous producers.

There was too much squandering and even more debauchery. Many had gotten rich overnight. Hundreds of men and women found themselves receiving the attention of the press worshipped by millions. The new idols threw themselves to luxury and pleasure in search of happiness with the help of their voluminous wallets, mansions, expensive cars, bootlegged whiskey, and orgies.

Suddenly, Hollywood could now boast of being the trendiest party city and, at the same time, one of the most corrupt places in the country. Many homosexual artists had to conceal their sexual preferences, and *"lavender marriages"* became customary. As it was, Oscar Wilde was married and had children, just like many other homosexual men of the time in Hollywood. Lesbians looked for social approval by marrying other actors like Marlene Dietrich, who married Rudolf Sieber, who lived 37 years with another woman.

Scandalous moral clauses began to fill artists' contracts, and movie censorship was constitutionally approved in 1921 in 36 states.

After the upheaval in media scandal brought upon the Arbuckle case, which was named after Roscoe *"Fatty"* Arbuckle, who was charged with rape and murder of an actress and was also linked to the death of William Desmond Taylor, the public became apprehensive of Hollywood. Producers panicked and created the *Motion Pictures Producers and Distributors of America (MPPDA)*, offering William H. Hays presidency of the guild. His new job came accompanied by an annual check for $100,000 dollars. And became known as the *"Tzar of Hollywood."* One of the first changes Hays executed was to include a morality clause within artists' contracts, in which stars promised to live a life free of any sort of scandal.

He was a pretty strict and repressive guy. His attitude left an imprint on the rise of the American film industry. Since 1935, censorship doubled with the creation of the Decency Legion, founded by petition of the Pope and American bishops. In 1967, it gave way to the new age classification system *MPAA*.

The Hay Code structured a supervision and censorship model that prohibited the screening of many European movies in America.

The lifestyles within the city were known nationwide thanks to the press. However, the underground world was still vastly undiscovered, riddled with sex and drugs, where all of those wishing to run from the imposed moral sense of society could hide easily. We were a fraternity, and only those whom we wished could join.

So many imposed moral codes, groups abiding for more decency in public life, wanted life to be quieter, more decent, and yet it almost brought on the contrary.

The homosexual and bisexual women of Hollywood got together in the *"Couture Circle."* A group that remained together during the golden years of Hollywood from 1920 to 1950.

Many of my lovers came from this circle, and many well-known actresses were part of it, too, but I would rather not disclose their names.

Women who had an active life as lesbians were part of this circle at some point or another, even those who just wanted in out of curiosity.

Needless to say, this circle remained anonymous since there were many groups in opposition to homosexuality being publicly known.

It became a tradition to hold small meetings in the house of one of our fellow friends, Greta, who always refused to participate in those encounters.

On the numbered occasions when she did, she kept her distance from me. She always behaved like an *Ice Queen* in public. Sometimes, she would leave this meeting accompanied by some beautiful girl or *"exciting secrets,"* as she would call them.

And I would be left submerged in the most excruciating episode of jealousy. Sometimes, I would leave by myself completely depressed. Other times, I would leave in search of love from another woman, though no one could erase Greta from my mind.

When I was born in Stockholm, it was a cold and ancient European town, and my world was reduced to the humble house where I lived. Hunger was the only thing that was constant in my home, and aside from the hunger, the cold never left us.

My father could have been the most loving parent. There was only one problem: he lived every day drunk, fighting and hitting my mom. My brothers and I lived among constant fights, screams, and beatings, hunger, cold, and scarce education. We could not afford anything else.

Ever since I can remember, I slept with my sister amidst the cold, the fears, and the fights. We got used to sleeping very close to each other in search of a sort of refuge.

One night, when we were teenagers, we camped close to the shore on Arsta Island. Since we grew accustomed to sleeping together, we slept together that night. I always felt safe in Alva's arms, but this night it was different. The night was different. Maybe it was the summer or knowing we were far away from home. But it woke our libido up, and we forgot our blood relationship, and with the recklessness that is so typical in teenagers, we started playing with each other.

It was not sex. It wasn't anything like what I experienced after with my other lovers or Mimi. It was an erotic game where two naive girls pretended they were grown women. Maybe we unconsciously repeated what we many times saw our parents do in the room we all shared. It was a game for us, a game with no consequences; we kissed each other without really knowing anything about kissing. We touched each other like my father would touch my mom on many nights. I don't look back on that memory with pleasure; I don't recall feeling any pleasure from our encounter. It was just a childish game. I can't say the same thing about that same summer when I left with my friend Eva and got a boyfriend, Gustav, where I finally knew what it was to have sex.

When he touched me for the first time, I convinced myself that a man's touch could never satisfy me. Maybe it was his lack of skills, but when he penetrated me, I felt used, like a simple object of his pleasure. He penetrated me, moving desperately in a mad career to reach orgasm.

Meanwhile, my encounters with Eva were different, filled with kisses, sweetness, and contact. Maybe it was Gustav's inexperience, but for me, it was not the same.

I did not enjoy it like I did with Eva. I saw them make love on various occasions while I enjoyed touching myself with my skillful fingers. Afterward, in Hollywood, I would very much enjoy it when I found my friends kissing each other playfully, without a doubt, enjoying being a voyeur.

When she finished shooting *"Mata Hari,"* she felt exhausted. She had worked in four different films during that year. She was completely drained. We needed to get away, so we headed to Santa Barbara, a beautiful Spanish-like city.

With the same architectural design you could find in Andalucía, Spain. With time, this city had become a sanctuary for artists. Far enough from Hollywood to become a refuge and oasis filled with peace. We strolled through Santa Barbara, holding each other arms without anyone being suspicious of my love for her. From far away, we seemed like two best friends or even sisters. We spent two weeks at the *Baltimore Hotel*, a hotel visited by many actors.

Like always, we chose different rooms. We went back to Hollywood, where she would return to film in 1932. She had two upcoming films to shoot, *"As You Desire Me"* and *"Grand Hotel."* The latter would make her win an Oscar for best movie of the year. Her phrase *"I want to be left alone"* would be remembered just as much as her popularity.

When she finished shooting *"As You Desire Me,"* she already had the next contract signed for *"Queen Christina."* The movie script was based on a story by a common friend of ours, Salka Viertel, and Margaret P. LeVino. To Garbo, playing the role of *Queen Christina* had been her biggest aspiration during her student days at the *Royal School of Acting.* However, she had plenty of time before beginning to shoot *"Queen Christina."* And time is very valuable when you are young, and the world is at your feet.

She asked me to accompany her on a long transatlantic trip to Sweden. She said I could help her get ready for her role.

How could I refuse? Was it even possible to say no?

All desire was to spend time with her. We left New York and boarded the *Olympic Transatlantic*. It would be a long voyage. Our first stop would be London, and then we would change boats and sail to Stockholm.

Whenever she finished shooting, she'd become a bit depressive. The sea enchanted her. Surrounded by the vast ocean made her feel like just another speck on earth. There, she felt far away from fans, the constant stare of unpleasant people, and the *"evil species,"* as she would call the press. The sea always comforted her.

As it was beginning to grow customary, she had her disguise on the whole time, trying to go unrecognized by anyone in the same boat. Her face was concealed behind ample sunshades, and her head was covered with a large scarf. She locked herself in her room and stayed there for three days.

While I began to regret accepting tag along on this trip. She did not come out of her cabin until the third morning when she went to the boat deck by herself. She rose very early; I still slept in my room, where I still continued to regret having embarked upon such a journey. I had nowhere to go until arriving in London. Two days later, when the shore was no longer visible. She left her cocoon completely renewed. She was back to being the delightful, seductive lover. She shined with her inner radiance. Like her cameramen, Cecil Beaton was quoted saying: *"To watch her is to face the most remote depths of the human face."*

She sat near the deck and let herself go in her beauty. A blue vastness behind her. After having breakfast, I found her and contemplated her in silence, afraid of interrupting her thoughts and making her mad. When she noticed me, she turned towards me and made a gesture that I guessed was a smile. Blushing by the heat of the sun's rays, she said:

"Good Morning, Sleepyhead. You missed one spectacular sunrise. Nothing compares to seeing the sunrise when you are on the ocean."

I had been sitting there for hours, I was hungry, and I had not had breakfast, but I was happy to be there. I quietly thanked God for allowing her to come back to reality. For a bit, I thought my illusion of spending time with her was completely lost.

"You are beautiful, and I really like how you look sun-kissed, and your eyes shine and scream that you are alive. Are you OK? Do you need something?" I asked. *"Do you wish to go back and maybe have fun inside your room? Do you wish to go back and have breakfast where you were seated earlier?"*

"No, let's have breakfast inside the room. I want you to kiss me. My ambition is to kiss you. Here, let's go to the room."

I was taken by surprise by the conversation and her motivation to continue our talk. She was almost unrecognizable. I ordered the breakfast to be delivered to her room, and when I got out of the bathroom, there she was, naked, hiding herself in a chiffon robe. Totally naked, she returned. I still do not know just how

wet I was from seeing her nude. My mouth was salivating, and I could feel a very strange and inexplicable sensation going down my back. She took my face between her hands, touched my hair, and pulled me close to her belly, and my hands wrapped her waist. I felt the happiest being in the world. Two tears left my eyes. No wealth could have paid for this moment. Without saying a word, she took me to her bed. I could not resist. I did not want to oppose it.

She undressed me slowly, like a virgin before a pagan ceremony. She explored my body with her kisses, kissing each inch of my skin, but she kissed my lips with exceptional desire.

My breasts became hard, and she ran her lips over them. She kissed my barren womb. I could feel the heat accumulating in my body. She turned me around. I pushed my face against the bed, biting the sheets with desperation. I felt her go over my back with her lips. Her hair grazed my skin and heightened the pleasure. She kissed and bit my bottom. I could feel her fingers separating each cheek to give way to her mouth. Suddenly, I felt her warm, hard, and sharp tongue exploring my deep caverns until she reached my genitalia. I could feel her mouth sucking on my clitoris and her mouth penetrating my vagina.

Everything in the room was spinning. I felt like the only human in the world to experience such an intense pleasure. Moaning and gasping for air, I orgasmed. Her fingers were inside of me and knew exactly the spot of my ecstasy. They began with slow movements, and then they went over my labia, arousing long-forgotten desires. My body was vibrating with excitement. I came on her hands, and she took them to her mouth. It was her pay for such skillful loving. She drank my love juices. When I thought everything was over, she kissed my mouth.

I could perceive my aroma and my own personal taste on her lips. We straddled each other and started rubbing each other. What a pleasure I felt. It was incredible, and we did not need masculine penetration. Our clitoris rubbing, our breasts coming close to each other, and wise movements of our hips made us explode in pleasure.

Garbo would not stop moving her hips. With each movement she made, I could feel her swollen clitoris rubbing on mine. We both orgasm. Who cares about what's next if you are loved by the being you worship, by a goddess of love, a sex expert. I kept still and lay on her lap like a girl seeking refuge in her mother's arms. Some time had gone by, and I'm unable to say exactly how many minutes had gone by, but I lay on top of her, and I started paying her back for the love she just gave me. The only time that mattered was when we made love. The only thing that matters is our intense orgasm and our willingness to give each other pleasure.

Now, life was back to normal. Even though she boarded under a fake name, many passengers stared at her with suspicion.

Was it the Hollywood Diva?

She wished to go unperceived, so when someone asked her:

"Excuse me, ma'am, are you Greta Garbo?"

Garbo would smile politely and say, *"I'm afraid you are mistaken; I am Miss Harriet, Harriet Brown."* She would immediately answer like she was reading from a well-rehearsed script.

During the trip, no public displays of affection were allowed, not even holding hands. Our rooms were separated. During the night, I would go visit her and return to my room before sunrise, like a lover escaping before the husband gets home. The year before, she spoke about buying an island in her home country, where she would retire from movies. The international press was all over that news, but nothing could be further from the truth. She had bought a house in the country for her brother and mother. However, she refused to help him get into the elite world of Hollywood. She vehemently opposed him pursuing that path.

"If I bring him to live with me, he will be a young boy with no worries, living at the expense of my name."

Maybe it was true; maybe she concealed the real reason. It might be that her brother was unaware of her real-life intimacies. Nevertheless, he acquired certain popularity in Swedish films thanks to his last name.

We finally reached Stockholm, an ancient European town with narrow and curvy streets that made car traffic almost impossible, even though it increased every day. A city that laid the same foundation it had 100 years ago. As soon as we settled ourselves in a rented house, we began her quest to find the loft where *Christine the Queen* had lived. She visited the *Skansen Museum* in *Djurgaden Island, the Royal Library*, and devoured an incomplete autobiography of the queen herself.

She read more than a thousand aphorisms; her letters, all there was left was for her to travel to the Vatican to recollect more of her memories.

In Stockholm, she was not as pestered by fans or the press as in America. She could calmly walk the streets in Stockholm. Barely anyone noticed who she was. Nevertheless, she never left her disguise. In every place she visited, she gave herself another name. Those who managed to recognize her smiled at her coyly and tipped their hats in the form of a salute.

She worked very hard during her stay. She tirelessly read French and Swedish while she went over them out loud with me. I was her secretary, her scribe.

Was I happy during my stay in Stockholm?

I could have been. But my happiness was never complete. There was something that smeared our ideal getaway. The ghost of her past relationship with Mimi Pollack ruined everything.

Many nights, I was left home crying bitterly while knowing Greta was running to Mimi's arms. They met on many occasions, sometimes spending the whole day together while others just spent the night together while I waited for her back home.

They would often make love in our bed. Then, I would escape to walk around town completely submerged in humiliation and pain. I would go back to the house with my heart completely broken, begging that Mimi would have left by then. But often, when I returned, she was still inside the room with Greta. I could hear their laughter, their words, and their moans. Both of them were submerged in affection, affection Mimi stole from Greta that belonged to me.

Mimi knew about our relationship, but she would show up and impose herself, not for one-second thinking about my pain, my tears, or how much suffering I was. In this play, she was the queen, and I was a timid damsel. *Was I humiliated?*

Yes, but there was nothing I could do. Love bears it all. It's really incredible how much similarity exists between Greta and Queen Christina. There is a quote by the queen that resonates so well in both of their lives: *"Solitude is the element that moves among extraordinary men."*

More than an aphorism, they were prophetic words for both women. They both left behind fame and wealth in search of pursuing the validity of their thoughts. Both women lived surrounded by people but remained completely alone. Both lived loving other women who did not correspond to their love.

The queen loved women, and the proof lies in the numerous letters sent to Countess Ebbe Sparre, *"Belle."* Belle married, leaving the queen hurt by her abandonment. Just like Mimi would leave Greta 300 years later.

Before her father's grave, she told me how much she would have loved him to see her success. They were both so happy in the memories she held. The joy and laughter he would react with when Greta talked about her dream of becoming an actress as a little girl.

After spending time with her mom, it was very difficult to say goodbye once again. Greta always remained in touch and would send her mother her monthly allowance, which would keep her living comfortably.

But her biggest pain, without a doubt, was saying goodbye to Mimi. Though she knew her love was not corresponded and perfectly knew they would never be together, she would never stop loving her.

I fell in love with Mimi Pollack, with a crazy teenage love taken over by the passion of a first love. Without a doubt, beneath her beauty, there lay a virginal soul.

She was very important to me at this stage; she was my lover, friend, and confidant. She fell in love with me before fame and before the spotlights. She came from a well-accommodated life. I was the poor girl. Mimi helped me and gave me her support. It was love we felt, not interest. She was not after the Hollywood Diva; she fell in love with the poor girl from a poverty-stricken neighborhood in Stockholm.

I left for America in search of a career as a movie actress. I left amidst the height of our relationship, and maybe if I had not left, we still would not have remained together. But knowing I left during the height of our passion left a void within me. I was separated from family and friends, and I missed her desperately.

The cultural difference was one of the biggest setbacks I encountered while forming myself as an actress. In those moments of despair, I took refuge in her memories to mitigate solitude and the sadness caused by a new and unknown life.

Arriving at the movie studio was a rude awakening for me. I was just a dull girl from the fields in Stockholm. I had no knowledge of etiquette. I was like a beast that rose in the jungle. But suddenly, I found myself in the middle of civilization. I gathered strength from this; it made me believe I could do it. I was able to make up for my shortcomings. I knew I first had to earn my place. When I was not shooting, I would be listening to the radio, trying to learn English.

And I did, even though my accent was very thick and almost gave off a masculine tone. After a while, I was able to go from working in silent movies to speaking movies due to my newly acquired English. People could now hear me talk and enjoy the movies.

It was a very hard and lonely phase in my life. All I did was work, study, and think about her. Loving her at a distance made me question whether she would one day return to me.

How could things turn out?

I was no longer the poor student girl. I would be a triumphant movie star.

We finished our stay in Stockholm and were going back to Hollywood. The trip back was a mix of joy, tension, fear, and pain. She would soon be facing the biggest challenge of her life. There was more she wanted than to depict a worthy rendition of Queen Christina.

On the way back home, she locked herself in her cabin studying the script. She had been out of the public eye for some time now, and she feared the public had forgotten her. But the thing she feared the most was being replaced by a new up-and-coming actress.

She went into her role as Queen Christina like it was her first time as an actress. Days went by without seeing each other.

Nevertheless, she would still call me on Saturdays to come to visit her. I would drive for almost two hours to Santa Barbara. Where I found her looking for refuge from the tension provoked by filming. When we got to the hotel, she plummeted onto our bed, completely tired, just letting me know beforehand that all she wanted to do was rest. You could tell she was experimenting with resting sleep since she would jerk.

Moving constantly while I only managed to hold her against my chest as if protecting her from an imaginary beast. To be a loving company for her was the biggest reward for me. Her work days were long and stressful. The dress rehearsals, the makeup, and the transformation into her character took long work hours. She was accustomed to being the undisputable diva. However, in this movie, she is a controversial character who behaves like a man without losing her femininity. She shot scenes of horseback riding and inside the royal stable, and in another scene, she was a queen taking care of state affairs.

She finally accomplished her goal; it turned out to be her best acting performance. She did not attend the premiere. I did for her. I was her eyes, ears, and mouthpiece. She waited for me back in her home, completely overtaken by pure emotion. She demanded to know each detail, each comment made by the public. It was not until a month after her premiere that she visited a small theater to see the movie. Completely in disguise, she managed to blend in with the public.

Salka Viertel never forgave me when I left her for Greta in 1930. She waited patiently for the perfect moment to seek revenge. Finally, the moment came in 1940. She stole me from the exclusivity of Greta's movie scripts and the leftovers of affection Greta would reluctantly give me. Over the years, we had held a sort of amicable friendship. But the whole time, she resented my betrayal. This time, she would betray me. She slept with Greta, too. My relationship with Greta was in shambles, and to give it the final blow of grace, Salka introduced me to Marlene Dietrich. She knew how much Greta and Marlene hated each other. But she meant this to hurt me and my relationship with Greta. In Marlene, I found a totally different woman. And couldn't help letting her seduce me. Marlene was a beautiful woman. Parallel to her beauty was her exquisite manner of treating those she cared for.

She would call me if she delayed filming scenes, she would send me beautiful love notes, and she gave me love and the sweetness I needed.

She did not produce heating passion in bed, but she did warm it up. She was not addicted to carnal pleasures like Greta, but her attentions were made up for the lack of passion.

We had an intense and beautiful romance, and I knew it wouldn't last long. Marlene was not used to settling down. But she allowed me to share my time with her. She was a woman who gave all of her love, and I was in need of someone like her.

She did not disappear for long periods of time like Greta. We would go out on long trips to the beach. She was not afraid of holding my hands when strolling on the shore. She laughed like a little girl, and it made me feel immensely happy. We made love freely, and nothing stood against us. After making love, we talked for hours. We sometimes talked about Greta, and she would laugh, telling me:

"You will never become the owner of her love, that dirty Swedish peasant. She

will never be happy or make anyone else happy. She lies and controls women as though they are her property."

I shared my bed with Marlene and Greta with Selka. They were together when Greta heard the news about my new romance. In a long letter, Greta recriminated me for treason. She waited for my eternal faithfulness. Greta ended up completely shutting me out of her life.

During my solitary waiting, submerged in tears and anguish, she expected me to be eternally faithful. The affair with Marlene had grave consequences. Greta would no longer take my calls or letters. The last one I sent her, she mailed it back to me completely unopened.

In a fit of frenzy, I decided to leave Hollywood. I could no longer stand being there. I was heartbroken, alone, and without a stable job. My contract as a screenwriter had not been renewed. My masculine mannerisms irritated the crew on set. The gossip that insinuated that I had the most beautiful woman in the industry on my bed infuriated them. Most likely because they would never even go so far as to have a drink or a glass of wine with these women.

They were like animals in heat, full of irrational hate and jealousy. I decided to return to the *Big City* and realign my life away from the chaos in Hollywood and its disastrous high couture groups. I wanted to restart my profession by going back to the theater and personal life by living far from Greta's selfishness.

Some months had gone by since my arrival in New York, and I was hardly thinking about her. I felt calm and relaxed. When suddenly, I received a letter from her asking me for a small favor. Without hesitating, I accepted, and without having so much time as to realize it, I ended up becoming her errand girl. I was mailing her articles she shopped for and managing hotel reservations. I am back to being a slave, but I was no longer paid with affection.

Convinced of not being able to continue this absurdity, I decided to make a radical change and left her for good. The Second World War had ended, and Europe was rising from the ashes like a phoenix. So I decided to have a long stay in Paris and other parts of Europe. During my stay at the Old Continent, I had an affair with Claris Charles Roux.

My last greatest romance I found was in Paris, far from New York. It was with Poppy Kirk (Maria Annunziata Santori), she had been raised in England and France. Poppy was another strange case in favor of my karma. She was a dream, a revelation that changed my life. We had met in Hollywood, but one night, I had a beautiful dream about her. This fantasy motivated me to find her.

We lived a nice relationship; we took turns staying in a loft in Paris and a beautiful house in Normandy. We were hostesses of a circle of women who loved other women.

However, Greta's complaints reached me all the way in Paris. She wasn't happy and would not let me be happy either. She sent me notes where she addressed me as a little boy once again.

"Tell me, little boy, have you stopped loving me? Have you forgotten about all the promises you made me?

Am I no longer the woman you swore to love all of your life?"

I responded to her desperate letters;

"Do you want me to go back to you? Then tell me so, and you will have me in your bed before dawn."

She is selfish. She thought if I was not hers, I couldn't be anyone else's. I knew perfectly that I didn't mean much to her. But she couldn't stand me being happy. She was playing around, hurting me, and humiliating me. She depressed me and left me more confused. Even thousands of miles away, she was a disturbing influence on my freedom.

I met Marlene Dietrich while filming *"Die Freudlose Gasse"* in 1925. We both were amateurs in the movie scene, and we both played secondary characters, playing the roles of two prostitutes. She was, without a doubt, a diamond in the brute. She had the skills I lacked.

My character was a hungry prostitute working the streets. She came to my rescue and, by doing so, ended up fainting in my arms. She touched me in such a gentle way, with an exquisite sweetness. She was so evident and real in her affection they decided to censor that scene. When the director called for a cut, she held me tight and lingered in my arms.

I wanted time to stop and continue being held by her far away from any disruption and from people who might decipher my innermost wishes.

The same day, in the shared dressing room, while I undressed behind the folding screen, she went behind it, too, to help me button my blouse. I was frightened and shaking, but she kissed my neck and ran her nails through my back. Then she followed the same trail with her silk-like lips.

While she muttered words in German that I could not comprehend. I did not say a word, nor did I do anything to resist me. She turned me around and locked her lips with mine. I felt I would faint; she dragged me to the house where she lived, and she got me inside her car, where she continued with her passionate lips. I had long forgotten about the driver or if he could see us and could no longer hear the horses galloping.

On her bed, I felt unique and loved by her special violinist's fingers. Fingers wise in knowing which strings would make me vibrate. She kept me in constant ecstasy. We held an intense affair over the course of a few weeks while the movie finished shooting. In the we parted ways, we did not keep in touch, and soon I forgot about her.

Many years later, we ran into each other in Hollywood, but we both pretended nothing had happened. Maybe she, indeed, had forgotten everything. I was just another lover in one of her movies. Orson Welles introduces us to each other, and I have an immutable smile on my face. There she was in front of me and had not aged one bit. I saw in her eyes the same joviality from 15 years ago.

Her fame had not quenched her desire for adventure and recklessness. She treated me with the same indifference as she had always done. Each time, she ended up putting up more walls between us.

Nevertheless, I never complained or asked her why. I very much desired her, but I hated her for making me feel used.

We both denied having met before. Until I had an affair with Erich Maria Remarque, not because I loved him. I was never interested in a man. But because she had had an affair with him, and I wanted to make her mad. When she found out, she was furious and called me an *"arrogant, selfish, untrustworthy filthy peasant."*

The distance between both of us was exacerbated by my senseless provocation. I still believed in love. I had cheated on Mimi with her. However, she ignored my pain, and I never spoke to her. I never kissed her again. Our movie careers grew like two parallel lines searching for infinity but never intersecting.

No doubt, I was very naive in the affairs of love in my first years. I gave myself into insatiable affairs that ended up hurting my feelings and shattering my illusions. Nevertheless, each wound made me stronger, and each tear hardened me. I grew up and convinced myself that I would never have the strength, to be honest about my sexuality. But it had toughened me up to the point that I knew I would never cry over someone. I would become a strong woman.

Was I happy or not?

I don't know. I always had someone waiting to have in my bed. All I had to do was a phone call, and I knew that person would leave everything to come to me. Many women would come to me in search of pleasure, some that were on my list of conquests and those I hated. I had others who only wanted to be docile slaves, those I hated too, and first on that list was Mercedes.

Mercedes was a one-night stand in one of the craziest nights of the craziest city in the country. The night Selka introduced us, I did not fancy her due to her masculine attire and her short-back hair. I never really quite understood why some women feel the need to imitate men.

It's hard for me to conceive women trying to act like men, dressing like men, and behaving like a man. I like being dominant in relationships. But I would never go as far as to insinuate that me being the man of the relationship. I have no wish to be regarded as a man. The only thing me and men share is our love for beautiful, feminine women.

Nonetheless, I was taken over by her freshness and boldness. She did not know my sexual inclinations, but that did not stop her from trying to seduce me while she handed me the bracelet she had bought in Berlin for me before having met me. Her intense green eyes, tanned skin, and gypsy-like appearance seduced me. It was like playing cat and mouse. She could have been just another acquisition, but there was something in her I liked. I have no regrets about having myself involved with her. I always held against her, having exposed me in her last letter, along with the names of many of her other lovers. It really surprised me, too, along with so many other names. I never imagined she would boast of having so many lovers.

While completely defaming their names along with mine. I have no doubt that she loved me. Better said she worshipped me. I was her greatest, most mystical, and maleficent love. A love that was toxic to her spiritual and mental health. Even though I was involved with many other celebrities, no one stood so much disdain from me as she did.

She was always willing to respond to my calling. She was in Paris with her new Hollywood lover, and all I had to do was write her a letter calling her my little boy, and despite my past behavior, she answered: *"Just tell me to come, and I will be on your bed before dawn, your wish is my command."*

Though we knew it was impossible to see each other before dawn, if I had told her to come across the ocean to see me in Hollywood, I'm sure nothing would have stopped her. She would sell her soul if it was necessary to just be next to me before dawn.

That was her. She gave everything, expecting nothing. Never complained; she just wanted my love, and I never gave it to her.

Why is love hardly ever reciprocal? Why do we love those who do not love us back and hurt us?

This is how I lived many intermittent relationships with Greta, where she always controlled everything. She would decide where we would meet and how many days we would spend together. I lived in constant wait for her call while she was in the middle of shooting movies. I waited for that call every day to go back to her lips and kiss her once again.

But she would never call back, knowing how hurt that would leave me. Yes, it's true we left on long trips together, but she also abandoned me for long periods.

Our affair lasted until 1944 when she finally decided to have me out of her life. She prohibited me from going to call her or to reach out to her by any means. She had expelled me from her life like she had done with Marlene in 1925. She even denied having met me when someone asked her for me.

Hollywood was the witch hunt started by McCarthy; everyone could have been subject to suspicion, from actors with left-wing views of the world to those with dubious morality. Once again, *"lavender marriages"* became the norm.

Some, like Greta, decided to disappear from the public eye. While a more rebellious bunch decided to face what was taking place in public life, just to be vetoed from any film project.

Europe had begun to heal from the atrocities caused by the Nazis. Paris was once again the city of light, and I lived my life on both continents. For a whole decade, I moved from city to city, sharing different beds with different women. I was loved by many, but I continued to love only one. I silently kept waiting for a letter from her where she would address me as her darling or little boy. But it was a sterile wait.

The last time I saw her was in 1957. She knocked on my door in my apartment in New York. When I opened the door, I almost fainted and was left speechless. It had been a while since I had had her close. Her beauty was fading; she was wearing a loose gabardine that covered her wrinkled attire. Her eyes, those eyes I loved so much, were lackluster, very sad, and dry. Without a doubt, she must have been in incredible inner turmoil to come to me. She pushed me aside to enter my house and immediately said:

"I have no one to take care of me. I am completely alone."

I was in the middle of the living room, not knowing what to say or what to do. A couple of minutes went by until I was able to react. While she was lying on a chair, hiding her sobbing with her hands over her face. I had never seen her this vulnerable. I slowly got closer to her and consoled her; she proceeded to cry over my chest. The same tears I had cried for her years back due to her disdain. I don't remember how long we stayed like that. All I remember is that it was already nighttime when she got up to use the bathroom.

"Don't leave. Stay awhile. I will make you something to eat, and we can drink a glass of wine. It will make you feel better. You seem very depressed."

She agreed to stay. She asked me if she could take a shower and change clothes at my house, so while she was taking a bath, I prepared dinner as fast as I could. I knew she loved to eat light dinners, so I like salads and or chicken. She took a long shower, and when she came to me, she looked much better, like she had recovered the vitality she had missed when she knocked on my door. We ate in silence in a candlelit room while we listened to Frank Sinatra.

"You were always so romantic."

Those were her cold words meant as a compliment.

I hardly cared what she said, if she insulted or beat me like before.

Now, she was in need, and I was her only hope. She stayed for the night and two more. I never left her. For I knew that when she recovered, she would leave and never come back.

We shared incredible moments; we were two mature women, both over fifty, experts in the affairs of love. We knew how to touch each other to take the other to the point of pure pleasure. She loved me, and I loved her with the intensity that I had done in my youth and with the wisdom that had come with the years. I kissed, and she pleased me, knowing it was the last time we might be together. I kissed her with bewilderment. And ran my lips over her aging body and dried breasts. I kissed her womb with desperation; her labia seemed like the wings of a butterfly. I kissed her intimately until she orgasmed. I drank her fluids. Her cum in my mouth left me immensely satisfied. Her once beautiful thighs were now just a memory.

Now, her fair skin was full of veins. We both rubbed each other with frenzy. The incessant rubbing of our clitoris led us to intense orgasms. To a long-awaited session of pleasure together. It had the power of all the hurt I had gone through all those years waiting for her. Her once strong and firm back was filled with small wrinkles; her once fair skin was now opaque, but I did not care, and I kissed her back with the same craving I had years before.

I still saw her as I did in Lake La Plata in Nevada almost 27 years ago. Or during our reencounter on our trip to Sweden. She kissed me intensely during those two days, we had sex orgies, and she sucked on me like she had before, she complimented my personal aroma, and she said it was her favorite from all the women she had been with.

Same to Jesus, she rose on the third day, like a sort of messianic vision. Similar to a slug leaving its shell, she emerged from her lethargic state. Without saying a word, she dressed herself in clothes that had been ironed and washed with infinite tenderness. I waited for the moment in which she would rid me of mine, my clothes that had dressed her in these past unforgettable days.

I watched with great devotion each of her steps as she put on sunglasses that hid her eyes. Which on this particular day seemed rather mournful. And her ample hat that hid most of her face, though she often used to say that *"Custom-made Italian hats were not designed to hide oneself,"* or maybe she was being honest when she said she *"could not stand the sun."*

She lit a cigarette, accompanied by her eternal companion: fear. I followed behind her in silence. Before leaving, she turned to me and grazed her long and cold fingers over my face in what she meant as a loving gesture. Coldheartedly, she muttered three words that would become our epitaph, three words that created a schism between us and separated us worlds apart.

I couldn't imagine this would be the last time I'd see her. It didn't seem possible for me to even think, *"I wouldn't speak to her again."*

"I'll call you."

She said in a whisper as she turned, almost disappearing at the elevator door.

I was ruined; I had nothing left from my golden years. I was a withered and sickly woman, 70 years old when I went back to live in Paris. I rented a small room where I played with the charity of my friends. I was desperate, and though that's not an excuse to justify my acts, I did not find any other solution to my misery but to write my memoir, in which I exposed my affairs with great movie stars. It was inconsiderate of me.

The few friends I had left turned their back on me. Which made me hit rock bottom. The earnings I had recollected were not enough to make a living on. By not speaking openly about all of my affairs, by having denied having affairs with many of them, and despite the excellent reviews, it had not reached the expected success. But it did not matter. Even though I did not openly confess the names of many, everyone knew who I was referring to. They themselves identified in my narrations, in each event and word used to describe the happenings.

No one wanted to hear from me, not even her. From that moment on, she hated me like never before. Like Peter, she denied having met me whenever she was asked if I was her friend or if she knew me when I was a screenwriter in Hollywood. She erased me from her memory as she did with Marlene.

I hadn't seen her in years, and our youth was but a memory. But there is not a night when she is not wandering in the room.

She still comes back every night, and we make love with the same intensity we had before. She still strolls around my room naked, with her confidence and smirk on her face, while she says loving phrases to me that I now realize were as fake as her acting. She was cold and scheming. I don't think she felt love for anyone, not even Mimi. All she felt was infatuation exacerbated by distance.

I don't think it was even possible for love to thaw her cold heart. I do not know if she ever loved anyone. I know she did not love me. But for me, she was everything from the moment I met her. I will always love her, and I will never stop. If life would permit it, I would repeat our destiny for eternity. And if I ever encounter her in another life, I will love her with the same passion and devotion.

My biography, or confessions of an old and sick woman, brought me the hate and disdain of those I exposed in *"Here lies the heart."*

It's my literary will, and in it, I confess many secret encounters. I was criticized for having exposed so many famous figures, but they were just part of my memoirs. I did not mean to do anyone any harm. It was just the reality I lived, my truth, and my affairs with many beautiful women of the period. I was hated and envied by many men, many of whom could not fathom me having their idols as my lovers.

Was I the most famous lesbian of my time?

I do not know. There are some things you cannot measure. This is one of them, but I am sure I loved and was loved by the biggest divas of my time.

I had on my bed great Hollywood goddesses like Marlene Dietrich, Alla Nazimova, Eva Le Gallienne, Isadora Duncan, Ona Munson, Katharine Cornell, Maude Adams, and Adele Astaire. During my life, I accumulated many lovers. From unknown stars that would soon meet fame to world-recognized stars, writers, and so on. My list has it all, and it includes names like writers Edith Wharton, Amy Lowell, theater actress Katharine Cornell, Dorothy *"Dickie"* Fellowes-Gordon, and Tamara Platonovna Karsavina, the beautiful Russian dancer. Even though she was married, we had an intense affair in 1920. We were friends and lovers. She was the only one who remained my friend after the publication of my memoir.

However, the pleasure I once experienced is now the burden I carry. Much has been said about me; much has been said about the friends and enemies I have had.

All that is left of me in them is a vague memory of me. In others, hate and resentment. They think I made it in Hollywood by dropping names and seducing, but that is a lie. I made it to the Mecca of movies by a recommendation of Marbury Elsie de Wolfe and my work as a writer, and yes, it is true I am living in complete misery despite having been raised in a wealthy family. But I squandered everything. I gave myself a life of luxury and pleasure. I did not think about my tomorrow. And now, my poverty is the result of my past debauchery. But I never went to bed with anyone for interest in making it as a successful writer or for any other similar motive.

Yes, I was a frenzied lesbian; I hit myself hard in the face with the stigmas imposed in my time and the double moral. For there were many women who criticized us with great zeal, and they themselves burned in passion to spend a night with a woman. Men never accepted me. They hated me because I boasted of my great loves. I used to tell everyone:

"There are no impossible women, just hard-to-get women."

It did not matter to me if a woman was married. I always managed to make her mine. Something that irritated the vanity of many men.

I used to wear red lips, and my short black hair slicked back with Vaseline, and I would dress myself in a masculine suit with a very big cape. This made some people call me *"Count Dracula."* Others called me *"the lover of stars."* They were right. I loved, kissed, and lived with many stars; many of them were idols in the sexual fantasies of millions of men in America, but in real life, they were mine.

A brain tumor destroyed me, and I died in absolute misery. I ended my days living out of charity after having experienced great opulence growing up. It was like a family curse. I was not the only one that died poor.

Much time had gone by since that day in 1957 when I left Mercedes' house after having spent three days together. Many years have gone by since she published her book when she spoke of her relationships with me and other women. Many years have gone by since her death, and every day, I'm more surprised by the things I see now. I feel a sort of nostalgia for Hollywood, not for the Hollywood that was in vogue when I was young, but the Hollywood I see now. Where there are no stigmas, prejudices, or taboos.

Everyone is welcome. Where people give themselves to crazy pleasures and are not criticized. On many of my lonely nights, I drove to Greenwich Village, a neighborhood known for its cultural and bohemian life. *"The Village"* had become the place for the *"Beat movement"* in the 1950s, the art galleries on *West 8th St.*, elegant cafes in *McDougal St.*, and the theaters on *Bleecker Street.*

An attempt to reproduce the Latin Quarter that existed in Paris for artists, *"The Happenings,"* and other artistic events that were less orthodox and bold took place in the Judson Memorial Church.

During the 1960s, a homosexual community formed in Christopher St. In 1969, a confrontation between the police and members of the LGBT community took place in what later became known as *"The Stonewall Rebellion."* This event is widely considered to constitute the single most important event leading to the gay liberation movement and the modern fight for LGBT rights.

I strolled slowly through its animated streets where couples formed by men and women walked together hand in hand, facing the death of the old value system. I would stop my car on the corner of Bedford and Grove, wishing to go into the gay bars without having to dress as *"Butch and femme."* They would not allow it, and I would not dare.

I wanted to go, knock on the door, and be received as a member of a secret society. I wanted to taste and experience what I had known back in my days: women dancing, enjoying a glass of wine next to their lover, screaming out loud their sexual orientation without fear. But after a while, I would just go back to my golden cage. I was always held back by the raid the police made in the gay bars. They would search everyone inside of them. If I was stopped by the police and taken to the station, my cover would be blown. I imagined seeing my picture on the cover of newspapers, with a footnote that revealed the motives of my detention. I could see myself walking to the Brooklyn Bridge before jumping into the cold water, trying to escape the scandal.

All due to my eternal fear of my preferences becoming public. Even though I knew it was known by many. I admire and envy today's divas who are not afraid to hide their true selves. I would like to think I would be just like them.

If I lived in today's world, would I be as bold as Jodie Foster, who has lived for over 15 years with producer Cydney Bernard?

Is it a repetition of my affair with Mercedes?

Is Angelina as insatiable as I once was?

If I could choose, I would like to be as courageous as Ellen DeGeneres and her beautiful wife, Portia De Rossi. I hope I don't make Ellen jealous by praising in this way the beauty of her wife.

I admire them, sure. I sometimes watch their shows and their crazy antics. They are so relaxed and fearless. Maybe I would be like them, or maybe I would still hide my true self like I did 80 years ago. Sometimes, I would have walked next to them on the streets of New York. And I continue to admire myself seeing couples walking hand in hand through the building I once lived in.

I see couples living, laughing, and loving in Central Park, not far from the places I used to walk myself, disguised with my loose gabardine, shades, and hat. I was never happy. Many women loved me, from Mimi Pollak, the woman I loved the most, to Mercedes, the woman who loved me the most.

Who forgave my disdain, rage, and coldness. Mercedes gave me love in exchange for nothing; she was always ready for me. To run to my encounter, to leave in trips, to honor me, and to give me love. I know perfectly that she gave me love like no one ever did, and I played her very badly. Mercedes allowed me to be free, to live, to breathe. If I had had the courage, I should have lived with her. I admire all those women who, without fear, tell the world their real preferences, who do not hide, women, who marry women, who love each other and live happily. *"Women"* is a great word, and it encloses too much meaning in its definition. Oh, how I admire their courage to face life and to go on.

It's a shame my fears were so great. How many opportunities did I lose out on being happy? The terror that provoked in me was the Hays Code, which prohibited any sexuality shown in films. The fear of the press pestering me if my personal life became public. Surely, Marlene, myself, and others missed out on a great opportunity to face the system that oppressed us. However, it's necessary to say that we stood up for our beliefs in the little way we could. She did it by dressing as a man and kissing a woman in *"Morocco"* in 1930, and I in *"Queen Christina"* in 1933, where I also kissed a woman.

Mercedes would not become a famous writer, and her contributions to the theater arts would not amount to much. Nonetheless, her story reveals a woman who stood up for her values and beliefs. Seldom did she take a step down. Even when her friends turned against her, she did not budge. She was considered one of the first feminists, and next to her friend Isadora Duncan, they fought to eliminate the imposed restriction for women to wear uncomfortable fashion. While some women still used tight corsets, Mercedes was wearing loose pants. She convinced me to visit her tailor once and to custom make me a masculine suit. One night, both of us wore our pants through Hollywood Boulevard. Causing great commotion. The next day, the press published the headline *"Garbo in pants!"*

She fought for women's right to vote, she lived as she wished, and she played the price. Her love for other women and her fight for acceptance was, without a doubt, the source of her originality and inspiration for writing.

Maybe her nickname *"the infuriated lesbian"* should have been a compliment allusive to her courage.

These were the first steps given, but we froze and remained static without progressing. We shut the door to the freedom that now exists; we were the pioneers of our time, and at the same time, we set back the freedom that we looked for and wanted for us.

I thank God for making me a woman. I thank him for letting me love them, forgive me for being so cowardly, and not have fought for my rights and freedom as they do now.

New Jersey, 2012.

www.ingramcontent.com/pod-product-compliance
Lightning Source LLC
Chambersburg PA
CBHW050550160726
48003CB00002B/839